CREEPS

Nobody is surprised to learn that there's a new girl in school — but they were when they met her! Kaybee Keeper not only wears weird clothes, she talks strangely too!

When she continues to behave so oddly, everyone can't stop themselves laughing at her. But there's something that makes Gwen and Jeff feel sorry for her. The others are all creeps for not making her welcome!

However, even Jeff can't help being curious, why won't Kaybee's parents say where they used to live? What kind of job did Mr Keeper have with the government? How can any *human* read as fast as Kaybee?

Is Kaybee Keeper really an alien?

CREEPS

An Alien in our School

Tim Schoch

Hippo Books
Scholastic Publications Limited
London

To my Mum

Scholastic Publications Ltd.,
10 Earlham Street, London WC2H 9RX, UK

Scholastic Inc.,
730 Broadway, New York, NY 10003, USA

Scholastic Tab Publications Ltd.,
123 Newkirk Road, Richmond Hill,
Ontario L4C 3G5, Canada

Ashton Scholastic Pty. Ltd.,
P O Box 579, Gosford, New South Wales,
Australia

Ashton Scholastic Ltd.,
165 Marua Road, Panmure, Auckland 6,
New Zealand

First published in the USA by Camelot Printing, 1985

Published in paperback by Scholastic Publications Ltd., 1987
Text Copyright © 1985 by Tim Schoch

ISBN 0 590 70625 X

All rights reserved
Made and printed by Cox and Wyman Ltd., Reading, Berks.
Typeset in Plantin by CH, Bromley, Kent.

ONE

Blah-blam! Just like that, summer was over and it was the first day of school.

As I walked to the bus stop the sun was shining, the birds were singing, I was wearing brand-new trousers and sneakers, and I hated every minute of it. I didn't mind going back to school all that much, it's just that I wasn't looking forward to facing *the* question. *The* question is the question everybody just has to ask you: "So, what did you do over the summer?" I didn't look forward to answering that question fifty million times. This year I decided to give everybody the same answer: "Nothing."

Gwen Sharp was already at the bus stop when I got there.

"Hi."

"Hi."

We had seen each other a lot over the summer, exploring or hiking or goofing around, so I knew she wouldn't ask *the* question. Gwen is tall and skinny with long, dirty-blond hair that always seem to be swinging around and sticking between her glasses and her face. She's my age, twelve. And she's a brain. She's so smart, actually, that her brain ought to be the size of a basketball. Her head isn't that big, though, and I doubt if it bounces. I like her.

"Well, Jeffrey, it's the start of another school year. Another year of challenges and friendship. Another year of learning and shaping our future. Another year of growing and—"

"Skiving."

"Right, J.M. A whole lot of skiving!"

Soon, good old scruffy yellow bus number 32 came leaning around the corner, filled with screaming kids. It stopped just past us with an awful screech. Some kid had blown a bubble against one of the windows, and it was stuck there with a wad of chewed blue bubble gum dangling below, like a person hanging from a parachute. We got on.

The usual kids were there. Some of them I hadn't seen since last June, and I didn't particularly want to see them now. Naturally a few of them asked *the* question. "Nothing" I said.

At school we piled off the school bus and joined the hundreds of other kids chattering their way to class. Both Gwen and I had Mrs. Binker this year, and when we entered the classroom, she was bouncing up and down on her toes behind her desk and checking everyone who came in.

"Name," she said to me.

"Jeff Moody."

She found my name on the list and put a tick by it.

She looked to Gwen.

"Gwen Sharp."

She checked off Gwen's name, then said, "Sit anywhere you like. I don't believe in alphabetical education. Sit where you are most comfortable."

We scanned the room. Only about half the kids were present. We said "hi" to a few of them and chose seats next to each other near the middle.

"Dave Larson."

I looked up. Mrs. Binker was ticking off the name of a slim boy with orange hair and a blizzard of freckles. He was Dave, one of my best buddies, and one of the worst practical jokers around.

"Hiya, Jeff, Gwen," Dave said, taking a seat. I was now between Dave and Gwen.

"Hi, Dave," Gwen said.

"Hiya, fire hydrant," I said.

"I told you not to call me that, creep," Dave said.

I'm sorry, his head does look like a fire hydrant, especially with his ears sticking out and his hair sticking up.

"Patricia Nickle."

We all looked up. Pinky Nickle was standing there bouncing on her toes exactly like Mrs.

Binker. The class began to fall about, but Mrs. Binker didn't know why. Pinky was smiling widely as she walked past me and took a desk at the back.

"Frederick McFink."

The biggest bully in the world was in my class this year! Great, just great. Most kids call him Crunch but not to his face. He got that nickname because of what he likes to do to kids. He rolled to the back of the room.

Soon practically everybody was there. Tandy Thomas, Gwen's friend, Mack and Lou, my other two friends, and fat Bob, who had managed to get even fatter over the summer. We were all chatting away and laughing and having a good old time. Dave was telling Gwen and me about the collection of dead flies he saved over the summer.

"Why would you want to save dead flies?" Gwen asked.

Dave chuckled. "To drop in people's soup and milk and stuff. It's a great joke, a great joke!"

I made a mental note not to eat with him all year.

"Kaybee Keeper."

The class immediately fell silent. None of us had heard that name before. She had to be the new girl in school. We all shut up to have a look.

"Class, class," Mrs. Binker announced. "I'd like you all to meet Kaybee Keeper. She's new to town, and new to our school. I hope you'll all make her feel at home. Kaybee, say hello to the class and tell us a little about yourself."

Kaybee made her arms go stiff at her sides as she turned to face the class. She smiled. "Hello, classlings. My name is Kaybee Keeper, and I am megahappy to be here in this school. Where I came from was so wonderful, it could take your face away. Whoops! I mean, take your *breath* away! Still and ultimately I feel ninety-two percent better being here with you." Then she bowed.

Everyone in the class looked at each other, then back at Kaybee.

Mrs. Binker swallowed loud enough for all of us to hear. "Thank you," she said. "Go on now, Kaybee, and have a seat."

It began when a laugh escaped through Dave's lips: *"Fffffffft!"*

That's all it took. The whole class fell about and started covering their bursts of laughter with their hands and whispering to each other between their fingers.

I'll tell you why. First of all, Kaybee was probably the strangest girl I'd ever seen. She was also the skinniest. Beanpole, really. She wore thick, white-rimmed glasses and had frizzy red hair that was uncoiling all over the place. But what the kids were laughing at—besides her wacky little speech—was her dress. It was a fluffy thing, bright orange, with red fish swimming around the edges of the sleeves and skirt. Blue bubbles from each fish

5

rose up and dotted the dress.

Even Gwen, who usually takes things calmly, gasped. Why would a girl dress like that? And who talks like that?

I caught myself shaking my head back and forth, back and forth, and laughing to myself. I couldn't believe what I was seeing.

Kaybee blushed and practically ran to the back of the room to the only seat left, next to Crunch.

"Nice," Crunch said, looking Kaybee's dress up and down and holding back his laughter. "Really nice."

Kaybee grinned at him. "Thank you, large one."

Mrs. Binker began rapping her ruler on the desk, and each time she whacked it, she said, "Now."

"Now, now, now, now, now-now! Enough. Time to start the new school year, and we are going to start it properly. Any objections?"

"Yeah!" Pinky shouted.

"You, young lady," said Mrs. Binker, "are starting the first day with a *D*."

Everybody else shut up fast.

"Now I want all of you to take out one sheet of paper. Right now! I want all of you to write on this topic: What I Did During the Summer Holidays."

Great.

I ripped one sheet of paper out of my notebook. I wrote one word: "Nothing".

Then I thought I might get into trouble for writing something so short, so I made it longer. Now it read: "Nothing much".

Gwen peeked over and saw what I wrote. She rolled her eyes and shook her head. I thought maybe I'd better start the school year on the right foot, so I began to write about my summer.

Half an hour later, while Mrs. Binker was collecting the papers, Gwen turned to me and started whispering. "I feel sorry for that new girl, Kaybee. Look at everybody, they're still staring and laughing at her."

"Yeah," I said.

Then, from my other side, Dave started whispering and chuckling at the same time. "Gorgeous, ain't she? Wow. Maybe the circus wouldn't let her change before she came to school! *Ffffft!*"

"Ha. Yeah," I said.

"Maybe," Dave said, "when she got up this morning, she was so tired that instead of a dress she put on the shower curtain!"

"Maybe," I said, trying not to laugh.

I wasn't sure how I felt about weird Kaybee Keeper. I mean, on one hand, what Dave said was true. She was pretty odd-looking. But on the other hand I felt sorry for Kaybee like Gwen did. There was something about Kaybee that was, well ...I don't know. I mean she looked and talked strangely, all right, but there was something else I rather liked about her, but I didn't know what it was until Gwen said it. "She's got dignity, Jeff." Yeah. Even though Kaybee was wearing a fish dress, she had dignity. Creepy dignity. Funny dignity, too.

"Kuh-why-yet!" Mrs. Binker shouted with three whacks of the ruler. "Thank you for the papers. You'll get them back tomorrow. Shall we begin? Miss Sharp, if you'll be kind enough to pass out the history books, we'll begin with a discussion about George Washington and the birth of our country."

It was going to be a long year.

Most of the rest of the day in school we didn't do much work. We just collected things. English books, maths books, biology books, social studies books, health books. You name it, we got it. I stashed them all in my hall locker until after school.

At lunchtime we learned that the price of cafeteria food had gone up, and most kids didn't have enough money. I noticed that Kaybee had brought her own lunch in a large, glossy, yellow paper bag. Later we got combination locks to put on the smelly lockers where we were supposed to keep our new, clean gym class uniforms. And after gym class, when we returned to Mrs. Binker's class, Pinky was whispering around the class that Kaybee had on red underpants with zebras. I didn't think that was funny—I had on Star Fighter boxer shorts myself.

After school was a riot. The kids were trying

to carry all their books home. They were staggering and weaving their way to their buses, dropping books and papers, laughing and shrieking and bumping into each other. What a mess. Gwen and I managed to get on our bus without an accident.

As we rode the bumpy number 32, we tried to talk above the screaming kids.

"Everybody will get used to her," Gwen said.

"Huh?" I said.

"Kaybee. Everybody will get used to her and not tease her any more. Don't you think so?"

"I doubt it."

"Maybe tomorrow she'll wear something a little more, a little more—"

"Normal?"

"Yes, normal. Hmm. I wonder where she came from."

"Beats me," I said. "Probably somewhere strange."

"I don't know, J.M. she certainly is an extraordinary person."

"Yeah, extraordinarily freaky."

"Here's our stop."

We swayed down the aisle, trying to balance our books, and made it down the steps and onto the pavement. The bus growled off. I took one step and dropped my books.

"Why do we have to put covers on these stupid things, anyway?" I said.

"To protect them, so kids can use them next year."

"It would be easier if they already came with covers."

"I like to cover them," said Gwen. "It allows me to be creative. To express myself. It's a challenge and it's fun."

"You're crazy, Gwen. I'll bet you and Kaybee would get along fine."

"Well, J.M., that's just what I have in mind. See you tomorrow." Gwen headed off towards her house, and I plodded home to mine.

As soon as I came through the front door, my little poodle, Igor, raced towards me, then attacked my shoe laces. I had to laugh. What a nutty dog. "Get out of here, you fuzzy freak!" I took a swipe at him but ended up throwing my books halfway up the stairs. I could swear Igor was giggling.

Then my kid brother, Joey, came flying out of the living room.

"Hi, Jeff! You should've seen what we did in school today! We each got a big piece of cartridge paper, and we had to draw the sun and moon and the planets from a picture in a book. But Arnie put a big smile with teeth on the sun and the teacher yelled at him! And then, when we went outside—"

"Joey," Mum said. Somehow she had sneaked up on us. "Joey, you can tell Jeff all about your first day of school later. Go on up and take off your new shoes."

"Gotcha," Joey said. He spun round and tramped upstairs to his room, jumping on my books as he went.

"And how was your first day of school?" Mum asked.

"Okay," I said. "You should see this new girl at school, Kaybee Keeper...." And as I picked up my books, I told Mum all about crazy Kaybee's fish dress and everything.

When I was done, Mum said, "I hope you're not making fun of this girl like everyone else, Jeff. Remember, everyone has feelings, no matter how strange you might think they are. I still remember when kids made fun of me—those kind of cruel things can stick with a person for a lifetime. So try to be nice to her. Who knows, she might turn out to be a new friends."

Somehow I couldn't picture myself making friends with anybody wearing a fish dress.

I went upstairs to my room and began covering my books. I tried to imagine myself dressing really weirdly and having kids making fun of me. I couldn't do it. I started laughing as soon as I pictured myself in a fish dress.

TWO

Kaybee covered her books with a wrinkly kind of black paper that had sparkling blue drops of water printed all over it. You always knew when Kaybee was opening her book because the crackling noise echoed all over the classroom—followed, of course, by giggles.

What was *wrong* with that girl?

I got a *B* on the paper about my summer holiday. Mrs. Binker made a big point of telling everyone that Kaybee got an *A*, the highest mark in the class. I think Mrs. Binker was trying to make us respect Kaybee or something, but it worked just the opposite. Now, not only was Kaybee cuckoo, she was also a *smart* cuckoo. The kids mocked her even more.

Nothing much happened until Thursday afternoon. I was sitting in one of the two large booths at Goggle's Candy Store, having my usual coke float made with bubble gum ice cream. With me were Gwen, Dave, Tandy, and Mack. Mack Buster is a really nice guy, big, lots of muscles and bones. He's an athlete, and like most athletes, he loves water fountains. They had a great water fountain at Goggle's, one of the old-fashioned kind, all white ceramic and tall. While I talked to Gwen and Dave, he walked over to the water fountain, bent over, and stood that way for a long time, letting the water splash over his lips. Then he rose with water dribbling down his neck, wiped his mouth on his sleeve, started to walk away, turned back, bent over and slurped some more, then came back to the table.

"Ahhh," Mack said, sitting down again.

"Why don't you get a water fountain for home?" Dave asked, laughing.

"Got one," Mack said, burping.

"Figures," Dave said. He leaned over and whispered to us, making sure that Mack could hear. "I've heard that Mack is half fish. It's true! Actually, his mother's a mermaid."

Gwen and I giggled.

"Impossible!" Tandy said.

"Funny," Mack said—he rarely says more than one or two words at a time. Every now and then his eyes glanced over, thirstylike, towards the water fountain.

"You know," Gwen said, "there are no such things as mermaids. Long ago, sailors sailing down south kept seeing these curvy creatures with wide tails and thought they were beautiful mermaids lying around in the water. But they were only manatees. A manatee is like a handsome walrus, but it does have a sort of womanly shape if you saw it under water or sunning itself on a distant rock, and—"

"What'd you do, memorize the encyclopedia?" Dave said, shaking his red head.

"I think it's fascinating," Tandy said. "You must know everything, Gwen."

Dave shook his head again and laughed. "Come to think of it, Gwen, you'd make a great mermaid. You look like a walrus!"

We all burst out laughing. Mack must have laughed so hard his mouth got dry, because soon he was walking back to slurp at the water fountain.

"Don't fall in!" Dave yelled after him.

"Don't you ever stop making jokes?" Gwen said. I think she was embarrassed. "Why don't you ever tell us anything intelligent? Do you ever read anything? Do you ever find anything interesting?"

Dave leaned across us again. "I find *that* interesting," he said. He gestured with his thumb towards the door.

In walked Kaybee Keeper.

Dave stifled a laugh.

Gwen shushed Dave and slapped his arm.

Tandy slumped down in her seat.

Mack gagged on the water and came back to the booth.

I stared.

Kaybee was wearing a bright green dress with a large apple tree and shiny red apples on the front. A robin was pulling a stretchy worm out of one of the apples. She knew us by now, and since Gwen and I were about the only kids who didn't always laugh in her face, she looked our way and smiled.

"Hey, Kaybee," Dave yelled. "Toss me an apple will you?" He laughed hard at himself: "Ffft-ffft-ffft!"

Mack nodded a lot—that's his way of laughing.

"Leave her alone," Gwen said.

Dave elbowed Mack in the ribs and said loud enough for Kaybee to hear, "Wait until a couple of weeks from now, when the apples start to rot!" He held his nose.

I had to laugh at that, and Gwen gave me a mean look.

Gwen motioned to Kaybee. "Ignore him, Kaybee. He's only kidding around. Come on over and sit down."

"No!" Tandy whispered.

"What's the matter with you?" Gwen asked.

"Nothing, just nothing. It's just embarrassing sitting with her, that's all."

"Don't be ridiculous," Gwen said, then shouted towards the door. "Kaybee?"

Kaybee held up one finger and walked up to the counter. Mr. Goggle, an old man with white hair, white shirt, white jacket, white trousers, and yellow teeth, smiled at her.

"Hello there," he said. "What can I do for you?"

"I would like one-and-a-half metres of red licorice whips," Kaybee said.

"Uh," Mr. Goggle said, "it doesn't come in metres, honey. Comes in packets. See? Six strands per packet. Each strand looks to be a little more than 30 centimetres. Suppose it might add up to two metres in all."

"But I am only one-and-a-half metres hungry," Kaybee said.

Dave was cracking up.

Mr. Goggle frowned. He was getting mad; *all* the kids gave him a hard time, I suppose. "Well, you'll just have to save some for later. Or give the rest away. Do you want it or don't you?"

Kaybee had to think about it for a minute. "Yes," she said, and Mr. Goggle began to stick the packet into a bag, "— I don't want it." Kaybee turned and walked away from the counter, and Mr. Goggle tossed the licorice whips back on the shelf and muttered something to himself.

Gwen nudged me to make room for Kaybee. "Sit down," Gwen said. "Want a lemonade or anything?"

Kaybee slowly sat down. "No, thank you."

"Well, I've got to be going," Tandy said.

"But you told me you had nothing to do," Gwen said.

"I, well...I just remembered something. Gotta go. See you tomorrow. Bye." And Tandy scurried out of Goggle's. Gwen looked puzzled.

Dave and Mack were exchanging elbow jabs,

and Mack got up to get another drink. Dave said to Kaybee, "You be sure to get a lot of sun. Apples need a lot of sun."

Kaybee looked right at him. "You remind me of the crazy people on the planet Solson. They live so close to the sun that their brains are constantly frying and sizzling. The only time they ever make any sense is during winter, when the weather is cold and the frying stops."

Dave just stared at her.

Gwen laughed and pointed at Dave. "That's one on you, Bozo."

Dave squirmed and tried to smile, then got up. "I'm thirsty." He went to the water fountain, where he and Mack exchanged drinks and kept looking back at Kaybee and shaking their heads.

"So, Kaybee," Gwen said, "how do you like our school so far?"

Kaybee sighed. "I feel like a Plutonian on Jupiter," she said.

Dave let loose a loud "Ha!" and Mack spat water all over the wall.

"Hey, you two, shut up, huh?" I said. How could they be so mean to Kaybee right to her face? I couldn't understand that, and it got me pretty mad.

"Thank you, Jeffrey," Kaybee said. "But they really don't bother me. It's like water off a drunk's back."

"You mean water off a *duck's* back," I said.

Kaybee nodded. "Duck's, too."

"That's right, Kaybee," Gwen said, "just ignore those idiots. You know how kids are. Dumb."

Then the door flew open and three girls practically ran in and sat on stools at the counter. One of the girls was disgusting Pinky Nickle, and it took her about two seconds to see Kaybee. She said something to the other girls, then slowly came over to our booth.

"Hi, Kaybee," Pinky said.

"Beat it," Gwen said.

"Why, Gwen, that's not nice," Pinky said. "I just want to see how Kaybee here is. How are you, Kaybee? These creeps bothering you?"

"No, not at all," Kaybee said.

"That's good," Pinky said. "If they ever do bother you, or if anyone ever bothers you, you let me know." She patted Kaybee on the back. "What are friends for?"

"And who is going to protect her from you?" Gwen asked. "Why don't you just beat it and stop playing games."

"Games? Is friendship a game, Gwen?" Pinky said.

"If it is," I said, "you're just lost, Pinky."

"Why I ought to knock your—" Pinky stopped and smiled. "Well, I can see I'm not wanted. See ya, Kaybee."

"Bye," Kaybee said. When Pinky was back with her friends, Kaybee turned to us. "You don't like her?"

"She's a creep," I said.

Kaybee shook her head. "She seems nice to me."

"Just watch out for her, Kaybee," Gwen said. "She's a troublemaker."

But I could tell Kaybee wasn't listening. Pinky was up to something. Even now Pinky and her friends were giggling, and I knew they were laughing about how Pinky had just made a sucker of Kaybee.

Soon Pinky and her friends left. Mack and Dave returned to our booth.

"Ooshy gracious!" Kaybee said, looking down at her teeny-tiny purple watch. "I have to get home now and get ready to look up."

"Look up what?" Gwen asked.

Kaybee stood. "Just look *up*," she said. "Bye bye." and Kaybee gathered up her books and headed for the door.

Dave and Mack each began scratching their heads.

"Oh, no," Gwen said.

I looked where she was looking. We could see Kaybee through the front window of Goggle's. Outside, all alone, leaning against a telephone pole, was Pinky Nickle. She smiled and walked towards Kaybee, said something that made Kaybee smile, and they walked off together.

"Oh, no," I said.

"I've got one question, Gwen," Dave said. "When you asked Kaybee whether she liked our school or not, she said she felt like a Plutonian on Jupiter. What the heck's that mean?"

"I think it means she feels like a stranger," I said.

"Exactly," Gwen said.

"Yeah, but who talks like that?" Dave said. "Who wears apple dresses? I mean she's so strange, it isn't funny any more."

I knew just what Dave meant. *Everybody* knew just what Dave meant. Kaybee had been in school only four days, and already everybody knew her name, what she was wearing today, what she wore yesterday, what weird thing she said to whom, and so on and so on. A change had even come over the class. During the first couple of days at school, the class would laugh and titter at every little thing Kaybee did. Now, even though they were still laughing, they were frowning too. They were puzzled. This girl, Kaybee Keeper, was *real*. She was serious, she was probably smarter than anyone in class, she didn't seem to be afraid of anyone, yet she was doing these way-out things. It didn't make sense. To me, and I think Gwen, too, it wasn't funny any more. Maybe it was a little sad. And maybe it was a little *too* strange.

THREE

On Friday morning I woke up with Igor licking my lips. I almost screamed and threw up and thrashed and died. Instead I threw off the covers and raced into the bathroom and ran my lips under the tap water until they began to get wrinkly. Yuk, disgusting.

I dressed and went downstairs to the kitchen and had breakfast with the family. The radio was playing some rock song with screechy violins and stuff. Dad was there, dressed in a suit and tie, sipping mud-coloured coffee. Mum was drinking tea, studying a sketch she'd done of fruit and making a few changes—she's an artist when she's not yelling at me or Joey or kissing Dad. Joey was sitting there in his underwear, slurping up porridge. Mum doesn't let Joey get dressed before breakfast because he's such a sloppy eater. Mum didn't notice the splotch of coffee on Dad's tie—even if she did notice, I don't think she'd make Dad eat in his underwear. It'd be funny, though.

"How's school, sport?" Dad asked. I knew he

meant me. He calls me "sport". He calls Joey "pal". I once called Dad "buckaroo" and he didn't like it too much.

"Fine," I said.

"How 'bout you, pal?"

Joey smiled with a mouthful of porridge. "Fine," Joey said. Some porridge flopped off his tongue and blopped down his chin.

"Joey!" Mum said.

I lost my appetite. I said my see-yas, got my books, left.

By the time I got to the bus stop I was going nutty. Mum had already taken out my itchy woollen winter socks, and I was stuck wearing them. I tried to scratch my foot through the sole of my trainer, but it didn't work. When Gwen came to the bus stop, I was sitting on the curb, whacking the bottom of my trainer with a big stick.

"What on earth are you doing, Jeffrey?" she asked.

"Feet itch. Wool socks." I went on smacking my trainer with the stick.

"Jog," she said.

"Huh?"

"Stamp your feet on the ground."

"Oh, yeah," I said. It sounded like a good idea. I rose and began stamping round the shoulder of the street. I was creating an impressive cloud of dust.

Soon the bus came grinding round the corner. By the time we got on I was out of breath from jogging. Stamping my feet helped the itching for a little while—about ten seconds. Then the itching got worse because my feet were sweating. Great.

When we got to school, either the itching stopped or my feet had gone numb from all the whacking and stamping.

Soon we were walking down the hallway, which echoed with the chatter of a couple of hundred kids. We passed Pinky, who was adding to the noise by yakking to a couple of her friends.

"And then Kaybee said, 'The sky is the exact colour of the grass on the planet Wurrwurr'. Can you believe it?" Pinky and her friends chirped and chuckled like chicks.

Gwen walked up to Pinky. "Hey, Pinky. Why don't you just leave Kaybee alone? Pick on somebody your own size. Make fun of me and see what you get."

"Beat it, Sharp," Pinky said.

"That's a warning," I said. I had to say something.

"Oh?" Pinky said. And she looked me up and down, then looked at each of her friends, and they all cracked up.

"I mean it," I said.

They laughed again. Gwen grabbed my arm and pulled me away. "It's no use," she said.

When we turned, we bumped into Dave. He was shaking his head. "Why are you two sticking up for Kaybee? You're just going to get into trouble, you know."

"With who?" I asked.

"With everybody," he said. "Come on, Jeff, Gwen, be real, huh? Kaybee's an oddball. Everybody picks on her. You going to fight everybody?"

"Leave it, Dave," Gwen said.

"Look," Dave said, pointing down the hall. "See what I mean?"

And here came Kaybee. The kids she passed stopped and stared, and after she went by, they covered their mouths and laughed. Today Kaybee was decked out in a starfield dress, a black dress with stars and constellations all over it.

Dave began making *fffft* sounds. I couldn't help it. My stomach started bucking, and I made light snorting sounds through my nose. Then, even though I wanted to stop, I began laughing in quick wheezes and sighs. Then, when Dave laughed out loud, I let loose with a couple of loud ha-has. But by then Kaybee was beside us. She stopped. She looked at me, and this really sad look scrunched up her face. She blinked a few dozen times, and her bottom lip began to stick out. Then she lowered her head and shuffled into the classroom. I wasn't laughing any more.

I felt like a slug.

Class dragged on and was more boring than usual. Every few minutes I'd look Kaybee's way, hoping she'd look at me so I could smile at her to tell her I was sorry for laughing at her. She didn't look at me at all.

The only interesting part of class that day was about forty-five minutes before lunch.

"Now, class," Mrs. Binker said. "Turn to page thirty-nine in your history books. We're going to have a little oral quiz."

"AWWWWWWW!" everybody said.

"Begin at the beginning of the chapter," she continued, "and read the next two pages to the middle of page forty-one. You have fifteen minutes, and when you're finished, I'll be asking questions about what you read. Everybody ready?"

"No!" boomed Crunch from the back of the room.

"We all know you are never ready, Mr. McFink. But ready or not, here we go. Begin."

I dropped my eyes to the page and began reading as fast as I could, trying to remember the names, dates, and places. I'd read about two and a half paragraphs when I heard a book slam and someone say, "Done".

Everybody in the class looked up. Kaybee was waving her hand in the air. "I'm done, Mrs. Binker."

Mrs. Binker looked at the clock, then back to Kaybee, then back to the clock, then back to Kaybee. "But Kaybee," she said, "it's only been four minutes. Even I couldn't read and absorb that much in four minutes. I think you'd better read it again, dear."

Kaybee shook her head. "But I have."

Everybody looked at everybody else and smiled and frowned and sniggered.

Now Mrs. Binker smiled. "All right, have it your way, Miss Keeper. What was the subject matter of the section you read?"

"The Boston Tea Party," Kaybee said.

"That's correct," Mrs. Binker said, smiling a strange smile. "Now tell us all about it." She sat back and crossed her arms, waiting for Kaybee to mess it up.

"Sure," Kaybee said. "It happened on December 16, 1773, in pretty Boston Harbour. The greedy British East India Company had been supplying the American colonists with lovely teas. The Townshend Acts of 1767 had put taxes on the colonists' tea and allowed the British East India Company to stay in business and sell tea cheaper than anyone else. The colonists were madder than Plyorian Zoonbugs. They didn't like any of it because they didn't want to be forced to buy tea from Britain, and they wanted a say in how and when they were taxed. So, soon the colonists felt they had to fight back, just like the secret Qui armies of the planet Bvig. They dressed up like Indians and sneaked aboard the unguarded British ships and destroyed 342 cases of tea by throwing them overboard into Boston Harbour. It was a massive planetoid protest and one of the main events that sparked the American Revolution and eventually led to America's freedom from the tyranny of England. There's a whole galaxy of other details if you'd like to hear them. Such as Paul Revere, who might have been with the colonists, and Samuel Adams and John Hancock, who were blamed for—"

"No, no, I think that is quite enough," Mrs. Binker said with her eyes popping out. "We could have done without your outer space gibberish, but still, it was excellent, Kaybee. Excellent, indeed."

The whole class started whispering. My mouth had gone dry, and I clucked my tongue around until it began to get wet. I could tell that even brainy Gwen was impressed by Kaybee's speed-reading display. We stared at Kaybee with everybody else.

Chalk up another weird thing for Kaybee Keeper. When we all calmed down and Mrs. Binker caught her breath, we moved on to geography, which was our homework from last night. We were told to memorize the names and locations of continents.

Kaybee bombed out in geography. For some reason she didn't know anything about where anything was on earth. She didn't know where any of the states were, or even where the United States was.

"Kaybee," Mrs. Binker said, "I just don't understand it. How can you instantly memorize all the information about the Boston Tea Party and yet tell me that you think Florida is in Greece? I'm baffled, Kaybee. Can you explain it to me?"

Kaybee looked guilty. She shook her head, shrugged, then blushed.

Oh, well, Win some, lose some.

Braaaaaannngggg!

Break.

We all dashed it out to the pavement, lawn, and trees at the side of the school. Immediately we split up into two groups—boys and girls. The girls broke into smaller groups and gossiped and chewed illegal gum. The boys slumped against the brick building or played catch or walked into the trees to fight.

Today I was a slumper, just slumping there and watching everybody else. I saw Mack, and guess where he was. Yup, the water fountain. His back is going to be permanently bent unless he finds another favourite beverage.

Then I felt someone come up and slump beside me. It was Gwen.

"Trouble," she said.

"Huh?" I asked.

She pointed. "Look over there, J.M."

I looked over there.

Over there was Kaybee. Two boys I didn't know very well had her backed against a tree and were saying all sorts of things to her I couldn't hear.

"Why don't we ease our way over there and see what's happening," Gwen said.

"Why?"

"Because, J.M., nobody else will."

"Okay."

We ran at top speed up to Kaybee, just in time to hear one of the boys say, "You're weird and you're ugly and you look like a *freak!*"

Kaybee yelled back, "I wish this tree was hungry, so it would eat you!"

Gwen and I thought that one over for a second before we took action.

"Hey! Hey!" Gwen hollered. "Cut that out."

"Beat it, four eyes," one of the boys said.

I made a fist and held it in the air. I have to admit, it didn't look too dangerous, but I continued, anyway. "I'll beat it. I'll beat *you!*"

Even though there were two of them, they began to back off. All mouth and no action, that's what they were made of. They were the kind of boys who don't fit in anywhere, who don't have any real friends, so they take it out on anyone they can. After a few more threats from both myself and Gwen, the boys wandered off.

I noticed that our little shouting match had drawn some attention. Dave, Mack, Tandy, fat Bob, and a few of our other friends were over by the fence, watching the whole thing. Most of them were shaking their heads. I wasn't sure if they were shaking their heads about what we'd done or what the other two boys had done. All I knew is that we had just stuck up for the screwiest girl in school—again. I felt good about it, though. It made up for my laughing in her face earlier.

"Thank you," Kaybee said. "Thank you,

both of you. You are heroes like the giants of Iiinin-Beta."

"Huh?" I said.

"Are you okay?" Gwen asked.

Kaybee shrugged. "I felt better once last summer. But I'm fine as can be now."

"Good, good," I said, wondering if my ears were blocked up or something.

Kaybee hung round with us for the rest of break. I noticed the other kids noticing, and even though I hated myself for it, I was kind of embarrassed walking with this spaced-out girl in the starfield dress. It didn't seem to bother Gwen.

Kaybee certainly did have a strange way of looking at things, I decided. With everything she'd said at Goggle's and in class and just now, I wondered how she came up with all that stuff. As we walked around she said, "Ooo, this is oceans of fun!" and "I wonder if that bird is my grandma?" and "Nothing is nicer than being with friends on a rainy day, and even though it is sunny today, it's still nice being with you."

Who says things like that? She was getting stranger every day! What was going on?

Braaaaannnnngg!

Time to go in. After Kaybee went into the classroom, Gwen pulled me aside. "Jeffrey, I've never heard anyone talk like Kaybee does, have you?"

"Yeah," I said. "In a science-fiction movie."

Dave passed us going into class. "Was that

Kaybee you were playing with, or do you have a new pet?" He chuckled at himself and entered the classroom.

"Same to you!" I shouted after him. I'm not used to being made fun of.

Mrs. Binker stuck her head out of the door. "Enjoying yourselves, you two?"

"Whoops," Gwen said. And we hurried into class.

After school Gwen and I found Kaybee sitting next to us on the bus. She didn't say much. She just sat there and stared at us, and every time either one of us looked her way, she smiled. I smiled back until my cheeks began to ache.

Even though we told Kaybee she didn't have to, she walked both of us home. First me, then Gwen. Yeah, I think Gwen and I had found ourselves a new freaky friend. Terrific.

FOUR

I guess Gwen and I were nice to Kaybee once too often. Now we were paying the price.

For the next two weeks Kaybee followed us everywhere. I mean everywhere. I mean, when I woke up in the morning, I expected her to pop out from underneath my bed.

It began one morning when I was leaving for school. I said goodbye to Mum and Dad and Joey and Igor and opened the front door to find Kaybee sitting on the front step. There were shiny droplets of sparkling dew in her frizzed-out hair, as though she'd been sitting there since about four in the morning.

"Kaybee," I said. "Um, what are you doing here?"

"A celestial morning to you, Jeffrey. I am your escort to the bus stop."

I couldn't believe it. She was waiting there to walk me to the bus stop. It was a good half-kilometre walk from her house to mine. But there she was with the early birds, all decked out in a bright yellow dress with a fanning peacock on the front. I didn't know what to say but came up with "Thanks".

So we walked to the bus stop. She strode along, swinging her books like it was the happiest walk she had ever taken in her life. And we did the same smiling routine—every time I'd look at her, she'd be looking at me and smiling. I smiled back, and she smiled bigger.

Gwen was waiting at the bus stop. She rubbed her eyes when she saw Kaybee and me walking up—I guess she thought she was seeing things.

"Hello, Gwendolyn Sharp," Kaybee said cheerfully. "I was Jeffrey's personal escort on this energetic morning. And tomorrow I will be your escort." Kaybee look back and forth between Gwen and me, as though she'd just told us we'd won a billion or something.

And sure enough, the next morning Kaybee waited for Gwen and walked her to the bus stop. And the next morning she met me. Then Gwen. Then me.

And that isn't all.

After school a few days later, I was sitting in the barber's chair at Hair Heights. I was facing the mirror, watching the barber trim the back of my hair when I saw some frizzy hair sticking up over the top of a magazine. Sure enough, there was Kaybee, sitting there with half-a-dozen shaggy-haired boys. She wore a brown dress that was printed with a wood grain like a log. She lowered the magazine and smiled at me in the mirror. The others looked from Kaybee to me, then raised their comic books over their mouths to hide their giggles.

When I left Hair Heights, she walked me home and showed me a hunk of my own hair she'd picked up off the floor. She gave it to me. "You might need this sometime," she said.

I stuck the hunk of hair in my pocket and managed a crooked smile.

And that isn't all.

That weekend, Dave, Gwen, Tandy, and I were up in Dave's terrific tree house. We were trying out the binoculars he got for his birthday.

"Wow!" Dave said. "I can see all the way to the school!"

"Lemme see!" Tandy screamed. Dave handed her the binoculars. "Oh! Everything's so big!"

"That's what binoculars are for," Gwen said, patiently waiting her turn.

"Yes, yes," Tandy said. "I can see the school. Heeee! I can even see my mother's car coming out of the shopping centre."

"Big thrill," I said. "Let me have a look." Tandy gave me the binoculars. "Hey! There's a flea on the roof of the school."

Dave cracked up. "A flea, sure."

"Yeah," I said. "It's wearing a little vest and a top hat."

Everybody laughed. We kept passing the binoculars back and forth, cracking jokes and looking all over the place.

Then we heard something scratching on the underside of the tree house.

"What's that?" Tandy said, backing herself into a corner.

"Probably a squirrel," Dave said. "Or a rat."

"A rat!" Tandy howled.

"Rats can't climb trees," Gwen said.

"You did!" Dave said, laughing so hard, he almost poked his eyes out with the binoculars.

The scratching sound came again.

"Somebody's down there," I said. "Somebody's climbing up."

"Well, this is a private tree house," Dave said. "No one else is allowed."

But it was too late. The trap door flew open. And up popped the head of Kaybee Keeper.

"Greetings from below!" she said. She was wearing a red-and-orange polka-dotted baseball cap with two brims, one front and one back.

"Sorry," Dave said, "only club members allowed."

"Oh, knock it off, David," Gwen said. "Come on up, Kaybee."

Kaybee eagerly climbed up into the tree house. She wore white-and-yellow-striped jeans and a gold sweat shirt that had the alphabet on the front in swirly red letters.

"Zipping Zeebees!" she said. "I've never been in a house tree before."

"A tree house, stupid, a tree house," Tandy said.

"Here, Kaybee, try these out," Dave said. He handed Kaybee the binoculars, which I thought was really nice until I looked closer—he handed them to her backwards.

"Ooshy gracious! Everything's so small and tiny!"

"Dave," Gwen said, "you really can be a jerk sometimes. Here, Kaybee, this is the way you're supposed to look through them."

"Oh," Kaybee said. "I liked them better the other way." She turned them round again, and Dave rolled his eyes.

Then we sat there talking. Everybody, that is, except Tandy, who was really rather snobby to Kaybee. Kaybee started yapping about all sorts of things. She said she got Saturn on her AM/FM radio. She said she liked to listen to running water talk, and to rocks sleeping. She said her favourite thing to do in the daytime was to count clouds. (Ever tried to count clouds? It's hard, believe me.) By the time she had finished talking, everybody couldn't wait to get out of the tree house because, I think, we were rather of scared of Kaybee.

During that two weeks Kaybee showed up in other places, too.

Like one Sunday afternoon. I took Kaybee and Gwen to my house for a quick sandwich. Mum was just coming down the stairs when we opened the front door.

"Mum," I said, " this is Kaybee Keeper. She's new at school."

"Keeper? Yes, we met your parents at the PTA meeting a week or so ago. Very nice parents. Hmmm. K.B.? What does that stand for?"

"No, Mum. K-a-y-b-e-e. Kaybee."

"Oh. Nice to meet you, Kaybee," Mum said.

"Hello, Mrs. Moody, nice to meet you, too," Kaybee said.

I was just glad she didn't say anything weird.

"Mum, we're going to make some quick sandwiches, then go back out, okay?"

"Sure," Mum said, "but don't make a mess. Come on, I was just making myself some tea."

In the kitchen Mum got out all the sandwich-making stuff, and we dug in.

Mum made her tea, but when she turned round to us, her eyes bulged when she saw what Kaybee was doing. "What are you doing, Kaybee?"

Kaybee was making a salami sandwich, trying to follow exactly what Gwen was doing. The problem was that Kaybee's sandwich had the salami on the outside and the bread on the inside.

"Whoops!" Kaybee said. Then she put the salami on top of the two pieces of bread. "Whoops!" Then she got it right.

Mum was blinking her eyes like mad. I was embarrassed and felt like crawling under the table.

We gobbled our sandwiches and beat it.

Gwen didn't seem to mind Kaybee hanging

around, and she didn't mind that all the kids laughed at us for letting Kaybee hang around. Gwen thought Kaybee was a brilliantly original person.

I, on the other hand, thought Kaybee was a brilliantly original wacko who was getting more wacko every day—but I had to admit that I was getting really curious about her. What made her tick? What made her tock? I had a strong urge to find out.

So, day after day, Kaybee kept turning up everywhere. The kids at school were still making fun of her, and one day, when Kaybee, Gwen and I were walking home from the bus stop, Kaybee started crying.

"Hey, what's the matter?" Gwen said, throwing an arm round Kaybee's shoulders. "Here, sit down. What's up?"

We sat on the curb. I didn't know what to say.

"I—I—I," Kaybee said. "I'm s-sorry. I hate being hated. I don't like not being liked. Oh, I feel lower than a space lorry with a flat tyre!"

"It's not that bad," I said.

"No, Jeffrey, it is far worse. It's worse than being a wart person. Why can't everyone be as nice as you two?"

Now that was a hard question. How do you tell a girl she looks and acts like a weirdo?

"Well, Kaybee," Gwen began, "the other kids aren't used to you yet."

"Why?" Kaybee said.

"You are rather different, you know."

"Everybody's different," Kaybee said.

"True, true," Gwen said, biting her lip, trying to think of something to say. She looked at me for help.

"True, true," I said.

Gwen glared at me and went on. "I mean, your life might be a whole lot easier if you wouldn't kid around so much by wearing these clothes and talking so strangely."

"Who's kidding around?" Kaybee said. She stood straight up, and her foot stamped down. "You both hate me, just like everyone else!" She tramped away a few steps, then stopped with her back to us. She hung her head. She raised her head. She raised her head even farther, so now she was looking at the sky. She turned back to us that way, then lowered her head and smiled. "I'm sorry. I'm okay now. My temper is sometimes my own best friend zapping me in the back. I know you are my friends. See you in the morning!" And she skipped away. Skipped, that's right.

"J.M.," Gwen said, "we've got to do something to help her. Her strangeness is getting stranger and stranger, and it's only going to get her into more trouble."

"And us. Kids are beginning to mock *us!* What do we do?"

"I don't know. There's something very different about Kaybee. Eerie. But I do know one thing, Jeffrey. If we don't do something soon, things will only get worse."

FIVE

Things got worse.

It was Monday after school. There was something wrong with our bus, and Gwen and I were waiting on the pavement by the car park with everybody else until a replacement bus arrived. It was boring. One reason it was boring was because Kaybee wasn't around. She had something special to do with her mother that day—a big, dark-blue car had come and picked her up after school.

"Hi, guys." Tandy Thomas came up to us, fluffing her blond hair and looking around. Her eyes are always moving around to see who's watching her.

"Hi, Tandy," Gwen said. "We haven't seen much of you lately. How come you don't come over any more?"

"I don't know," she said. "Where's Kaybee?"

"Went home," I said. "Her mother picked her up."

Tandy sighed and smiled. "That's good."

"You don't like her, do you?" Gwen asked.

Tandy shrugged, looked round to see who was looking, and said, "Not much, I guess." Tandy started shuffling her feet and fussing with her books. Something was on her mind.

"Coming over Wednesday night?" Gwen asked.

"Where?" Tandy said.

"To my house to watch T.V. *Invasion of the Slug Giants* is on. It's a classic."

"I forgot," Tandy said. "Yes, sure, Gwen, I'll be over, only... only...."

"Only what?"

"Will Kaybee be there?"

"I don't know, Tandy," Gwen said. "Maybe I'll ask her. Should I?"

"No!"

"What's wrong with you?"

Then Tandy sighed and began talking. "You know, we're good friends, Gwen, we really are. But kids are starting to make fun of me because I hang around with you because you're hanging around with that strange Kaybee."

"Who cares what the other kids think?" Gwen snapped.

"I do. I hate people making fun of me."

Just then Dave and Mack wandered over with one of my other friends, Lou. Dave was smiling, and Mack looked very thirsty.

"Hey, Jeff," Dave said. "Where's the nutcake?"

"Knock it off," I said.

Dave smiled again. "I promised Lou here I'd introduce him to Kaybee. See, Lou can't decide what Hallowe'en costume to wear, and I thought maybe meeting Kaybee would give him some excellent ideas."

"What's up with you creeps?" Gwen asked.

"We're not the creeps," Tandy said. "Nobody's making fun of *us*."

"Yeah," Dave said, "we're not the ones who are no fun any more."

"You saying we're not fun any more?" I said. Mack nodded.

"Bingo," Dave said. "The whole school thinks you and Gwen have freaked out. They figure that you've caught whatever strange disease Kaybee has. What's the matter with you, anyway?"

I was beginning to get steamed up.

Tandy suddenly stepped over and hid behind Dave.

"What's the matter with you?" Gwen asked.

"It's Pinky," Tandy said. "She sees me. She's laughing at me."

"So?" I said. "She laughs at everybody. She's a jerk."

"She thinks you're the jerks," Tandy said.

"Who cares?" Gwen said. She glared at Tandy. "You care more about what Pinky thinks than what I think? Are you going to let a hollow-head like that run your life?"

"But she's making fun of me!" Tandy said, stamping her foot like a three-year-old.

Dave threw his arm round my shoulder. "I'm telling you, Jeffrey, old bean, that things would be a lot easier on all of us if you'd kind of cool it with Kaybee. Come on, we're your best friends. Who cares about a crazy girl who dresses like a comic strip?"

I shrugged his arm away. I could feel my face getting red and hot with anger. "You don't know what you're talking about!" I screamed.

"Hey, easy," Dave said, backing away with his hands up.

"So, why do you think we're hanging around with Kaybee, anyway, huh? So we can be made fun of? Huh?"

"Why *do* you hang around with her?" Tandy squeaked.

Everybody, Gwen most of all, was staring at me, waiting for an answer. If I said I didn't know why we hung around with Kaybee, we'd be laughed off the face of the earth. Oh, no, they were laughing at me already, and I couldn't stand it. Somehow I had to really *show* them.

"We...I...uh..." I said. "Why would Gwen and I hang around with Kaybee? I'll tell you. For a *good* reason, that's why. But I promised Kaybee I wouldn't tell anyone her secret. And I'm not telling you. That's all I'm saying, and if you don't like it, *tough!*"

"A secret?" Tandy said, her eyes popping. "What secret? What secret could Kaybee have?"

"He's bluffing," Dave said.

"Why would I bluff?" I said. "You think I've been hanging around with Kaybee all this time just so I could bluff you? Come on, Dave, use your brain."

"Yeah," Mack said.

"Hey, pretty good," Lou said. It was the first word he'd said the whole time he was standing there. He's a short, rather square-shaped kid. "I knew there was something about that Kaybee that I didn't understand, and I didn't understand it because I wasn't supposed to understand it because it was a big secret."

"Okay," Dave said, acting really cocky, "let's discuss this a minute, Jeff. You say you've been hanging around Kaybee because she has this big secret. What kind of secret?"

"A secret secret," I said. "I'll be able to tell you soon, but I can't tell you now. I can't even give you a hint. I wouldn't tell anybody for a million dollars."

"Gosh," Tandy said.

"Bus," Mack said pointing. Sure enough, our bus was lumbering into the car park.

Before we got on, Dave grabbed my shoulder. "You'd never catch me being friends with Kaybee, no matter how big her secret was. All I can say is, Jeff, her secret had better be good."

On the bus I could hear Tandy telling Pinky all about Kaybee's big secret.

Great. I really did it this time. Naturally there was no secret. But by tomorrow morning, everybody in school would be dying to know what it was. And sooner or later I'd have to tell them what the big secret was.

We got off the bus and Gwen walked me back to my house.

"Well, J.M., now what?" she said, shaking her head. "You've got yourself in so deep, there's no way out."

"I know."

"When the kids find out there's no secret, we'll really have no friends."

"I know."

"This is going to take all our brain power to figure a way out."

"I know."

"How are we going to do that?"

"I don't know."

"Well, I do," Gwen said.

"Huh?"

"Jeffrey, sometimes you amaze me. Sometimes your sheer stupidity brings out you hidden insight and intelligence."

I thought that might be a compliment. "Thanks. What'd I do?"

"You said Kaybee has to have a *reason* to act the way she does. So far we've come up with nothing but guesses. Don't you see? There has to be one solid *reason* that would explain everything. And if we could find out her secret *reason*, J.M.—"

"We'd get our friends back!"

Yeah, the plan was good. Nobody does

anything without a reason, and Kaybee had to have a darn good one. And if we could find that out, my friends wouldn't hate me any more.

I had a chance, just one chance, to get my friends back. There was only one catch. What if Kaybee didn't have a secret?

SIX

On Wednesday evening, about an hour after dinner, I went up to the small attic room where Mum does her painting. I walked up behind her. Specks of red, blue, and yellow paint were flecked on her hands and hair. She was concentrating on painting faint little dots on a lemon. She does oil paintings of fruit, vegetables, and stuff like that, all arranged so that they form the face of a person. The lemon was somebody's nose.

"Mum," I said.

"Ooo!" Mum said. She jumped. "Jeffrey! Look what you made me do! My lemon's smeared. I've told you a thousand times not to sneak up on me like that. Knock! Always knock first!"

"Sorry," I said.

"Well, what do you want?"

"Just wanted to tell you I was going over to Gwen's to watch that film tonight, remember?"

"Yes, I remember. Couldn't you have told your father without bothering me?"

"He's asleep on the couch with Igor."

"Oh. Okay. Have fun. What time will you be home?"

"Let's see. The film starts at seven, so I should be home by nine."

"Good. Be careful. Now get out of here so I can finish my lemon."

"Bye."

"Go!"

Mum does have a temper when she's painting. I guess most artists are like that.

I hopped on my black dirt bike and rode through the strip of woods to the other side of the development to Gwen's house. I rang her doorbell, and she answered the door with a long face.

"Tandy isn't coming," she said.

"What happened?" I asked, following Gwen into their play room.

"Beats me, but she called and said she couldn't make it. Know what I think?"

"What?"

"I think she thought Kaybee was coming so she cancelled them."

"Probably." Gwen had asked Kaybee but Kaybee said she couldn't come because she had to look up.

"Who needs her?" Gwen growled, and flicked on the TV. "So, Jeffrey, Hallowe'en's coming in a few weeks. Have you thought about what you're going to be?"

"Something ugly and scary," I said.

"Oh, you're going out as yourself?"

"No, I'm going out as *you*!"

"Ha, ha, ha."

Gwen and I watched the ugly Slug Giants as they began to invade earth. Soon we started talking about Kaybee.

Gwen got down to business. "The key to Kaybee's behaviour lies somewhere in the things she's been doing, agreed?"

"Right."

"Now, what has she been doing? Dressing oddly. Saying strange things. Ah ha!"

"What?"

"The speed-reading, J.M. Maybe that's a clue."

Gwen was really impressed by Kaybee's speed-reading. Not very many people are better than Gwen at studying and remembering things. So while the Slug Giants landed in Central Park in New York and scared about fifty idiots, I began to wonder how a daffy girl like Kaybee could be an excellent speed-reader yet be so slow to catch on that she's making a fool out of herself by dressing like a nut.

"Maybe," I said, "Kaybee is crazy. A lot of very intelligent people go crazy, you know."

"True," Gwen said, "but I don't think she'd be at school if she were insane."

"Yeah. But maybe her parents don't know it."

"They'd know."

"Maybe they're crazy too!"

"Forget it, J.M. Too far out."

"Yeah."

Gwen got us a couple of cokes, and we stretched out on the floor and stared at the television in silence. The Slug Giants had just kidnapped the president when I got an idea.

"I've got it, Gwen. There's only one answer, there's only one reason why we can't explain anything about Kaybee."

"What's that?"

"*We're crazy!*"

Gwen laughed and laughed until coke started coming out her nose. She coughed and snorted and finally calmed down.

"Oh, boy, J.M. Warn me next time, okay? Woo!" She thought a minute. "You know, I think I've got the answer."

"You do?"

"Yes. Kaybee is just eccentric, that's all. She's brilliant, eccentric, and very shy. And because of all that, she feels very uncomfortable round everybody else. She's just showing off, that's all."

"Why?"

"To get attention. Make friends. Maybe she likes you, Jeff. Maybe she has a crush on you and is trying to get your attention."

"Ha. She's got my attention, all right. She's got everybody's attention. Gwen, I really don't think that's the way normal kids try to make friends. If you wanted more friends, would you act like that?"

"I don't have to," Gwen said. "I have all the friends I need."

That was true. Gwen had all the friends she needed. Until the next Saturday.

SEVEN

Saturday at last. It was a booming, beautiful sunny, crisp, and absolutely perfect day. I felt electrified. It was the day of the big football game, and I could hardly wait.

Today the meeting place was my house. It's at somebody else's house every weekend. Everybody would meet here, stock up on water bottles, coke, and a few snacks, then all of us would hop on our bikes and ride like a parade over to the field behind the school. It was great.

The game was set for ten o'clock, and Gwen was the first to arrive at nine-thirty. She had on tatty jeans, black sneakers, a faded red sweat shirt, and her hair was pinned up behind her head, making her neck look about as long as my arm.

"Today, J.M.," she said, "we're going to kill 'em!"

"You bet."

"Last time they beat us by one idiotic touchdown. But today we'll knock their socks off!"

Joey stumbling into the living room, rubbing his eyes. He's a late sleeper. "Can I knock their socks off, too?"

"Sorry, Joey," I said, "you're still too young to play. But you can watch or be water boy if you want to."

"I don't want to. Besides, I'm playing with Frankie today, so I can't come. So there!" And Joey stamped out into the kitchen.

"Hi, Gwen," Mum said from the kitchen. "Would you like some orange juice or anything?"

"No, thank you, Mrs. Moody."

"Jeff," Mum said, "I've been meaning to talk to you about Kaybee. Why doesn't that girl know how to make a sandwich?"

The 'phone rang. Saved by the bell. Mum answered it. She covered the receiver. "Jeff, it's for you."

I walked over and took the 'phone. "Hello? Yeah. Yeah. Yeah. Yeah. Okay. Bye." I hung up, went back into the living room, and flopped into the chair. "Mack can't come. Says he's got a cold and his mother won't let him out of the house."

"Oh," Gwen said. She looked as disappointed as I felt.

The 'phone rang again. Again it was for me. I listened and hung up. "Tandy can't come. Something about eating too much last night."

"Oh."

The 'phone rang again. And again. Soon we

didn't have enough kids on our team for a game, so I had to call the rest of the kids and tell them the game was off. They didn't seem disappointed at all. But I felt like dirt.

"They hate us, Gwen. They don't want to play because they hate us."

"Don't be ridiculous, J.M. Things like this happen all the time. Coincidence, it's called. Besides, my mother said a bug is going round. Anyway, the radio said it's going to rain this afternoon. We probably would have had to cancel it, anyway."

"Yeah."

"Cheer up. We've got the whole day ahead of us. You don't really think all our friends hate us that much, do you? Come off it, Jeffrey! School is one thing, but our football games are something else. No one would ever miss a football match for anything, you know that.'

"Yeah, I guess you're right." I was feeling a little better.

"So what do you want to do, chum?"

"The Zoo?" The Electronic Zoo was the best video game arcade around.

"Great idea! Could you lend me some money?"

"Sure. Let's go."

I raided my money box, and Gwen and I hopped on our bikes and headed for the Zoo.

Just zooming along with Gwen lifted my sagging spirits. There would be other Saturdays and other games. Right now, what I wanted to do more than anything was to beat Gwen at Thumper. She always kills me at Thumper. But not today! No way!

We screeched to a halt at the main road, looked both ways twice, and I popped a wheelie and we raced into the centre of town. Gwen laughed her head off when I took the corner too sharply and nearly crashed into the curb.

Now we were on the road that led past the school and straight to the Zoo.

"Race?" I said. I pretended my bike was a motorcycle and revved the handle-bar accelerator.

"You're on."

And we were off. I pumped my legs like I never pumped them before. Gwen's hair came undone and was flapping behind her like flames. We were even with the school when, together, we slammed on our brakes and skidded to a stop in a huge cloud of dust.

We just stood there for a moment, stunned out of our minds. And for the first time in a very long while, I felt like crying.

The game was on.

Mack had no cold.

Tandy's stomach was fine.

Nobody had the bug.

All our friends were out there on the field playing their hearts out, yelping with joy, shouting and screaming and having the time of their lives.

Without us.

Gwen and I looked at each other silently. Gwen gave me a handkerchief from her back pocket. I used it.

We turned our bikes round and began walking back.

Neither of us said anything. There was nothing to say. We both knew what had happened.

When we reached the centre of town, I just sort of stopped. All the energy I ever had was gone. I stood there, staring at the dust, not thinking of anything except the aching in my gut.

Then I saw a pair of green and silver and pink sneakers step up beside my bike. I looked up. Kaybee Keeper was smiling at me.

As usual lately, Kaybee had found us. And, to tell you the truth, I was glad to see her. At least we still had one friend left.

EIGHT

Kaybee's smile gradually shrank.

"You have long looks like a road," Kaybee said. "Is there anything I can do to make them shorter?"

I felt like telling her: *Well, for starters, Kaybee, you could talk like a human being.* But I didn't. What I did say was: "I need a float."

"Want to come to Goggle's?" Gwen asked Kaybee.

"Yes," she said quickly.

"Where's your bike?"

"Bike?" Kaybee said.

"Bicycle," Gwen said. "Don't you have a bike?"

"No, I don't. I don't know how to balance one."

"You can't ride a bike?" I said. It was the most ridiculous thing I ever heard. *Every* kid knows how to ride a bike. I know kids who know how to ride a bike but don't even *have* a bike.

"I feel like walking, anyway," Gwen said.

So we walked to Goggle's and settled

ourselves in one of the booths. Soon I had my coke float made with bubble gum ice cream. Gwen had her usual strawberry milkshake. Kaybee had a float, too—vanilla ice cream and diet ginger ale. Yuk.

I sipped my favourite drink in all the world, up through the straw and into my hot mouth. Ahhhh.

Kaybee squirmed excitedly in her seat before she spoke. "Did you see Venus last night?"

"Huh?" I said.

"The glorious planet Venus. It was sparkling bright red last night. Wondrous."

"No, I missed it," I said. I went back to slumping over my float.

"Jeffrey, Gwendolyn," Kaybee said, laying a hand on each of our arms, "what is troubling you? I know it is something implosive because you are always cheerful and sunny. If I can help, I will."

"It's nothing," Gwen said. "Just some problems with our friends, that's all."

"Big, lousy problems," I added.

"Rotten problems," Gwen said.

"Really crummy."

"Hateful."

"Idiotic."

"Inexcusable."

"The creeps!" I suddenly said, a little too loudly. Mr. Goggle, who was behind the counter, turned and looked.

"I knew it," Kaybee said. "It *is* implosive."

"You know what they did?" I said. "See, today we were supposed to play football with them. Well, they called and said they couldn't make it. Then Gwen and I were riding to the Zoo, and we saw them playing the game, anyway! They lied!"

"Why?" Kaybee asked.

"Because," Gwen said, "they have decided that we are not worthy enough to be their friends any more."

"Why?"

"It doesn't matter," I said. I couldn't tell Kaybee it was partly because of her. "They're not my friends any more."

"And we don't need them," Gwen said.

"That's horrible," Kaybee said.

"Know what I feel like doing?" I said. "Running away. Just packing up and hitting the road. Why stay where I'm not wanted or liked?"

"Oh, but you're wrong," Kaybee said. "You are liked by other kids. Your parents like you. Your teachers like you. I like you. I will be your friend always, and your friend, Gwen, for every minute for the rest of our lives and further."

"Thanks, Kaybee. But don't worry, Jeff's not going to run away," Gwen said. "But I do know how he feels. Haven't you ever felt like running away from home, Kaybee?"

"Yes. I ran away from home only once."

"You did?" I said. "What for? What made you run away?"

Kaybee shook her head. "I will tell you at another time." She stared into her float.

Running away must have been a big event in her life. I decided not to question her about it, even though I was bursting a gut to know.

Then Pinky Nickle walked in and right to our booth.

"What a lovely day!" she said. "I was just out for a walk and saw all of you here and thought to myself, hey, why not go in and say hi. Yes, it sure is a great day—a perfect day for football, right, Gwen, Jeff?"

I looked up into Pinky's puffy and smirky face. "Why don't you just beat it."

"Sure, sure," Pinky said. "It's none of my business if you decided not to play football today." She giggled a little.

Gwen stood. She looked like she was going to throw the entire booth at Pinky. "I'm in no mood for you, Pinky. Better leave."

Pinky began to back out of the door. "Right, right. I'm going. Guess I'll go over and watch the game. It's a great one today, too! See ya, Kaybee." And Pinky strutted out.

"That girl is going to get it one of these days," Gwen said. Then she turned to Kaybee. "See what I mean? See how cruel Pinky can be? She's no good, that twit."

"She's nice to me," Kaybee said. "But why did she come all the way over here to tell you about the football game?"

I couldn't believe it. Kaybee didn't see how

Pinky was trying to be mean to us.

"Forget it," I said.

"Excuse me for a millisecond," Kaybee said, and she headed for the girls' room. Gwen rose and went with her.

Then I noticed a folded piece of blue paper on the floor. I thought maybe Pinky had dropped it. Maybe it was a love note from some slob to Pinky, or something secret like that. If it was, it might be my chance really to get back at that stupid girl. I bent over and picked it up. I opened it.

It was the weirdest letter I'd ever seen in my life. It definitely was not Pinky's. Here's what was on the piece of blue paper:

Dear 15-R-Q,
I hope you received the §Rß*OL=+. I will send the X(9)33030-V-7 and the B??0jL-44z soon. Things are still ohHaa[!] and L38+Mn%§t2i. More later. Say hello to 13-V-G.

Love 11-K-B

I tried to work it out, to break the complicated code, but got nowhere. But just before Gwen and Kaybee came back, I worked out who wrote the note. The letter was written to 15-R-Q, so I guessed that must be a code for a person's name, maybe a person with the initials R.Q. If that was true, then the person who signed it at the end used initials, too. K.B. Kaybee.

To me, Kaybee had just stopped being a strange and nutty girl. She had bounded into the bizarre world of The Twilight Zone.

When Gwen and Kaybee were back in the booth, I showed Kaybee the note, trying to act as naturally as I could.

"Hey," I said with a laugh, "look what I found. Wonder who dropped it?"

"Let me see," Gwen said. She took the note and barely had time to look at it before Kaybee snatched it out of Gwen's hand.

"It's mine."

"Oh, really?" I said. "If I'd known it was yours, Kaybee, I never would have looked at it. I'm really sorry. By the way, what kind of note is it?"

"I'm sorry, I cannot tell you," Kaybee said, stuffing the note deep into her pocket.

"It looked like some kind of code," Gwen said. "Is that what it was?"

"Code, language, it doesn't really matter," Kaybee said, blushing furiously. "It's just some correspondence to some club I joined, that's all."

"Club?" I said. "I love clubs. What kind of club?"

"I can't tell you," Kaybee said, "It's a secret club."

"That's why the letter is in code," Gwen said.

"It's not a code," Kaybee said. She was getting a little too upset about the whole thing.

"It's...it's...oh, forget it, please. And I must be going. I will visit each of you, or see you in school, or something! Bye!" And Kaybee hustled out of Goggle's.

Gwen and I sat there looking at each other.

"Jeffrey, old friend," Gwen said, "this might be the clue to Kaybee's whole secret."

"Could be," I said.

"Probably is."

"Most likely it is."

"It *definitely* is"

"So, when do we start?" I asked.

"Right now!"

NINE

During the next week a lot of things happened.
Some little things, some big things, and one
whopping thing.

One of the little things that happened was
that the leaves were changing to orange, red,
gold, and yellow. Autumn hit fast and hard.
Also, Hallowe'en decorations started popping
up all over town. The school windows were
already filled with scary pumpkins, evil
witches, angry ghosts, and snarling black cats.
I'd begun work on my Hallowe'en costume,
too. I was making it myself, and I made sure
that everybody knew it was a big secret. No one
would get a look at it until I was done. The
secret of it all was driving my family bonkers.

Another thing that happened was that it
rained just about all week. It started as a heavy
plop-plop rain, then went down to a light
drizzle that looked like tiny flies zigging and
zagging all around. I'm telling you all that
because it created a foggy mood round my
investigation of Kaybee Keeper. I felt like a

detective, Sherlock Holmes maybe, and I tried not to miss any clues—I didn't actually *find* any clues, but I don't think I missed any, either.

My ex-friends kept bugging me for the big secret about Kaybee. In fact, the only time they ever talked to me was to make fun of me about this big secret I swore I had. I knew if I could find out (or make up) that secret, I would get my friends back.

Naturally Gwen didn't agree. She didn't think our ex-friends were worth it. She also didn't think we'd get anywhere by asking a lot of questions round school. What she thought was best was to watch Kaybee constantly and try to ask her questions. I told Gwen that that hadn't got us anywhere before, but she wanted to keep trying.

Meanwhile I talked to everybody I could think of—kids, teachers, even the school secretary, who said that background information on any student is confidential. I tried to convince her that I was a private dectective, but it didn't work.

After a couple of days of doing all that, I was stuck in a rut, up against a brick wall and getting nowhere fast.

"I told you so," Gwen said. "It's not going to do any good asking a bunch of questions round school. You're just making a fool of yourself, J.M. Teachers are getting mad at you. Besides, nobody knows anything. I'm telling you, we have to somehow get Kaybee to blab, to open up and tell us about herself."

"Yeah," I said, "tell us why she wears those silly dresses and talks the way she does and writes letters in code and follows us around and everything."

"That's the idea."

"I think it's a stupid idea," I said. "She's never going to tell us all that. We have to get a clue here, a clue there, then put it all together to get to the bottom of this."

"Jeffrey, you have no clues. You've even run out of questions. What else is left?"

"We need a break in this case," I said.

And that's exactly what we got. First a little break, then a megabreak.

It started in art class.

Outside, the rain was falling at though it was never going to stop. Mr. Evosco, our art teacher, a great guy with thick, dark hair that hung over his forehead, had given everyone a project to do at home. We were to draw a landscape in pencil. It was due today, and we all brought in our artwork wrapped in plastic to protect them against the rain.

"I can't wait to see what you little geniuses have done," Mr. Evosco said. "I'm going to wander round the room and spend a little time with each of you and look over your artwork. While I am doing this, you are free to talk if you wish."

So he began walking round.

"What did you do?" Gwen asked me.

"Wait and see," I said. I'm always embarrassed to show anybody anything I've done. Some kids like to show everybody everything they can do. Not me. Why? I don't know. I suppose I'm afraid of being laughed at or something.

"Ahhhhh! Yes!" Mr. Evosco said. He was standing in front of Pinky's drawing and holding it out in front of him. "Please, Miss Nickle, what is it?"

"A baseball field," she said.

"Ahhhh. Well, my dear, your perspective is a little bit off. Home plate looks as if it is sitting on top of the pitcher's mound. Here, let me show you what you should do." And he bent over and began sketching for Pinky, who began making faces behind his back, cracking everybody up. When Mr. Evosco was done he said to Pinky, "You enjoy making fun of people, Miss Nickle, don't you? If I wanted to, my dear, I could go down to Mrs. Johnson's class and find a drawing far superior to yours. I'm sure everyone here would get a chuckle out of that, but I won't do it. I won't do it because I believe that if you took a little more than five minutes with this sketch, you might have achieved something very fine." Pinky blushed, and he moved on to the next kid.

Soon he was at Gwen's. "Ahhhh. A desert. Very good, Miss Sharp. But what is this smudge back here?"

"A mirage," Gwen said.

"Ahhh. Well. Here, I'll show you a technique to make it look like a mirage. A few heat waves, like this, and a little shimmer, like this."

Then Mr. Evosco was holding my picture up in front of him. It was a drawing of the tops of all the roofs in the neighbourhood.

"Ahhh," he said—once we counted all the times Mr. Evosco said "Ahhh" during one class, and he said it seventy-three times. "Not what I would call a landscape, Mr. Moody. A roofscape perhaps. This is quite an ambitious undertaking, very difficult even for accomplished artists, and yours could be much better, but I appreciate your imagination. You rose to a respectable challenge, Mr. Moody, and I'm proud of you."

I grinned and bopped a little.

Finally Mr. Evosco got to Kaybee. And for once, he didn't say "Ahhhh."

"Good grief!" he said. He said it loud enough so that the whole room immediately shut up and looked his way. "Miss Keeper, this is, ... this is... How did you think of something like this?"

Kaybee shrugged. "It is what came into my mind."

Mr. Evosco turned towards the class. "Class. I'd like you to take a look at this drawing done by Miss Keeper. Though a bit odd, *this* is a landscape." He held up Kaybee's drawing.

Some kids giggled. Some went bug-eyed. Some rose to get a closer look. I thought it was the cleverest drawing I'd ever seen.

It was a landscape all right, but of nowhere on earth. The ground was filled with round holes and went back and back to strange-looking mountains with three peaks each. The bushes had stripes and thick leaves that looked like hands. The trees had no branches except way up on top, where two branches stuck out with drippy stuff at the ends. There were two suns in the sky. And here and there, behind a bush, beside a tree, were alien creatures that looked something like lit matches with three arms. To tell you the truth, it was beautiful.

"Miss Keeper," Mr. Evosco said, "you have much talent, young lady. What was your inspiration for this creation? Where does it take place?"

"It is a small planet in the Milky Way," Kaybee said. "A peaceful planet called Ooggeer, where the sun never sets because there are always two in the sky, two for day and two more for night. The striped bushes smell like sugar canes. The wet trees drip sugar water. And the creatures do nothing but scamper about and keep all those round holes clean, because out of those round holes, from the centre of the planet, comes fresh air."

Most of the kids collapsed at that. I did too. It sounded silly, and a little crazy. Mr. Evosco didn't think so.

"Quiet, please," he said. "Imagination is the key to artistry. Observation is the cornerstone. Put both together and you get a piece of art that is original. Before you ever put pencil to paper, you should learn a lesson from Miss Keeper here. You must *always* know your subject totally. You must know it so well that you feel as if you have lived there. Ahhh, thank you, Miss Keeper, for making my day. May I hang this in front of the class?"

"Ooshy gracious! Thank you," she said.

Right after school Gwen and I began our intense questioning of Kaybee.

"Where'd you get the idea for that drawing?"

"How long have you been interested in strange planets?"

"When did you start wearing clothes like this?"

"Where do you buy them?"

"Did you wear them where you used to live—where did you say that was?"

"Why don't you wear other clothes if you don't like kids making fun of you?"

"How do you come up with all those great lines, like the hungry bush?"

"What were your friends like where you used to live—where did you say that was?"

On and on we went, trying to sneak in as many questions as possible. But Kaybee wouldn't answer any of them. She'd shrug. She'd sigh. She'd say "I don't remember" and "It doesn't matter" and "I don't know".

But then she said something that knocked our socks off: "Would you two like to come to my house tomorrow? Maybe we can have lunch."

"Sure!" Gwen said.

"Maybe we can look up together!"

Oh boy, oh boy. I couldn't wait until tomorrow. We'd see where she lived. We'd see her very own room. Now we'd meet Kaybee's parents. We'd ask them a million questions. We'd find out what "looking up" meant. And we might, just might, find out the secret behind the bizarre behaviour of Kaybee Keeper. Then I'd be off the hook with my friends! Yaaay!

TEN

That evening I hammered awhile at my Hallowe'en costume, then went down for dinner. Dinner was great. Meat loaf, mashed potatoes with gravy, and sweetcorn. Dad had baked some bread—my favourite kind of bread—so I made some sandwiches. A meat loaf sandwich. A mashed potato sandwich. Then a sandwich with both and some sweetcorn. Joey thought he was cute when he made a bread sandwich. Mum thought we were disgusting.

"Daddy," Joey said, "Jeff won't show me his Hal'ween costume."

"He wants to keep it a secret," Dad said.

"Nobody sees it until Hallowe'en night," I said.

"No fair!" Joey whined.

I grinned at him with all the teeth I could.

"By the way," Mum said to me, "if you need any help with that costume, I can show you how to sew the hems, or double-stitch, or something."

I shook my head. "Trying to trick me into showing it to you, huh?"

Mum giggled. "Well, I tried."

I couldn't get to sleep that night. I tossed and turned and flung and flipped. My mind whirled with thoughts about Kaybee and everything she'd done, about Dave and Mack and Tandy, about the horrible day we were left out of the football game, about Mrs. Binker, about art class, about mashed potato sandwiches.

Soon, though, I conked out. I dreamed I was a bolt of lightning, shooting myself down and grabbing Mars bars out of Goggle's Candy Store.

When I woke up the next morning, I yelled. Something cold and smooth was pressed onto my upper lip. I looked down at it. I saw inside my nostrils. It was a mirror.

"Gooood morning," Gwen said. "I was just checking to see if you were breathing. You know, like the detectives do?"

I yawned loudly with a bark at the end, then clawed a hard hunk of gunk from the corner of my eye. "Gwen, what are you doing in my room?"

"Your Mum said I could wake you up, lazy bones. Let's get a move on. We told Kaybee we'd be there at eleven. It's after ten now."

I rose, dressed, ate a bowl of cereal, washed it down with a tall glass of orange juice, told Mum and Dad I was having lunch at Kaybee's, and left the house with Gwen.

It was a gorgeous Saturday morning. The sun was flashing all over the place. And there was a little nip in the air—either that or a bug bit me. The dog next door started barking. I barked back. Gwen thought that was funny.

We hopped on our bikes and rode across the street, through a couple of back gardens, through the strip of woods, and up and down and round a few more streets.

"What if Kaybee's folks are crazy, Gwen?"

"Not that again."

"Really. What if they capture us or something, or make us wear those weird clothes?"

"Don't be a fat-head. We'll just have to wait and see."

We didn't have to wait long. In a few minutes we were walking our bikes up the steep hill to Kaybee's house. Soon we stopped and stared across the huge, green front lawn to her towering, old, gleaming white house.

"Absolutely splendiferous," Gwen said.

"Great," I said.

The house was both. It had a huge front porch with white pillars. It was three storeys high and as wide as half a football field, counting the three-door garage attached to the right side. The roof peaked in three small windows. On top of each peak was a silver rooster weather vane. All three chickens were facing to the right, as though they were looking at something. I looked to the right but nothing was there.

We parked our bikes, walked across the spongy lawn, climbed the steps, and rang the doorbell.

Kaybee opened the door. She wore a jumpsuit that looked exactly like a huge piece of notebook paper, white with thin blue lines. She was excited.

"Slipping Sloothers! Hi! You're right on time, as usual!"

As usual? This was our first time there, so how could we be usual?

"Come in," she said, "and leave your troubles in the trees."

I'd left my troubles at home, and I wasn't about to go home and get them and stick them in her trees, so I just followed Gwen inside.

Right away I was surprised and shocked. So was Gwen. Why? The house was normal. To the right was a normal dining room with a normal table and chairs. To the left was a normal living room with a plain brown carpet, a nice comfy settee, fluffy chairs, a rocker, tables, lamps, and pretty curtains—it was so normal, it was almost boring. Right in front of us was a wide staircase curving to the left.

"Come in and sit," Kaybee said. We followed her into the living room and sat down. Gwen sat in an overstuffed easy chair and I sat in the rocker. "I'll be back in a minisecond," Kaybee said. She called, "Mummer! Dadder! They're here!" And Kaybee disappeared down the hallway.

"Warm, comfortable," Gwen said, looking around the room.

"Yeah," I said. "Maybe this isn't really Kaybee's house. Maybe it's just—"

"Oh, be quiet."

Then I got the biggest shock of all when Kaybee returned with her parents. Her parents were normal. Very normal.

"This is Gwendolyn Sharp and Jeffrey Moody. This is my mother and father."

"Hi," I said.

"Hello," Gwen said.

"How do you do," Kaybee's father said, shaking my hand. He was a short man with a balding head. He was pudgy and wore smallish glasses that kind of sunk into his eye sockets. He had a really friendly smile.

Kaybee's mother smiled and blinked her eyes. She was taller than Kaybee's father but only by about two centimeters. She was pudgy, too, with rosy cheeks and light brown hair that hung straight to her shoulders then suddenly curled.

I still couldn't believe it. I was expecting two out people dressed in aluminium foil or something. But here were two everyday, average older people who were dressed like my own mum and dad.

"Please, sit down," Kaybee's mother said.

Everybody sat down. It was like visiting my aunt, sitting around in a stuffy, boring house until you started yawning and falling asleep. I hoped we wouldn't sit around too long.

We kind of smiled at each other for a few minutes. My eyes kept jerking back and forth between Kaybee's weird dress and her parents' boring clothes. They didn't even seem to notice how their daughter was dressed. Odd.

"Your parents are very nice people, Jeff," Kaybee's father finally said. "We met them at the PTA meeting the other night. We hope to see more of them."

Big deal, I thought. I nodded and smiled.

"We met your mother, too, Gwen," Kaybee's mother said. "She said your father was out of town on a business trip. He works with computers or something, doesn't he?"

"Yes," Gwen said.

"Dadder used to work for the *government*," Kaybee said proudly.

"I'm retired now," said Kaybee's father.

He sure didn't look that old to me.

We sat in silence for another minute. Nobody knew what to say.

Then Gwen spoke. "Did you see Kaybee's picture? The whole art class really loved it."

"Really?" her mother said.

Kaybee blushed. "It was one of those pictures you don't like very much, Mummer. About planets and things."

"Oh," her mother said, nodding. She looked at us. "Funny. Ever since Kaybee was born, she's been doing things like no other child. She has her own mind, our Kaybee does. Her own style of doing things."

"That she does," her father said.

Silence again.

"Was your government job in Washington?" I asked. I was hoping he'd tell me where they used to live.

"Oh, no. It wasn't that important, no."

"Where *did* you used to live?" Gwen asked.

The Keeper family looked at each other. Kaybee said, "No place you've ever heard of."

Silence again.

Mr. and Mrs. Keeper certainly were quiet people. Shy, almost. Whenever I looked at them, they looked away. Mrs. Keeper kept twisting the handkerchief in her hands. Mr. Keeper kept studying the room. I came in here thinking I'd be asking them a million questions about Kaybee, but that's not how things were working out. They were really hard to talk to. But still, I couldn't understand how they could act so normally with this strange girl, their very own daughter, sitting in the living room wearing an outfit that looked like a sheet of notebook paper.

I guess Gwen was thinking the same thing, because she asked, "Mrs. Keeper, do you make Kaybee's dresses?"

Mrs. Keeper definitely got mad—she held it in, but I could tell she was mad because her face grew red and her lips grew thin. "No, I do not. Kaybee dresses as she wishes. And now, I think it is time for lunch. Let's go into the kitchen, shall we?"

We did.

Bright sunlight splashed all over the kitchen through three huge windows. We all sat round a round, glass-topped table to eat. Lunch was good, with plenty of food, and even though we didn't talk much, I enjoyed myself. Kaybee, however didn't eat what we did. She had her own special food that she called "health food". Believe me, nothing that looked like that could be healthy. Square blobs of white stuff, little balls of black stuff, long, stringy, clear stuff. Yuk.

"More milk?" Mrs. Keeper asked me.

"No, thanks. Lunch was great." I'd had two peanut butter and jam sandwiches and some crisps.

"Yes, thank you for lunch," Gwen said.

"Well," said Mr. Keeper, wiping his mouth with a napkin, "I suppose you kids would like to go and play now. Thanks for coming over, Gwen and Jeff. It was a pleasure meeting you. If you'll excuse me, I have some things to attend to in the study."

"Nice meeting you, too," Gwen said.

Mr. Keeper smiled and left. Kaybee rose to help her mother clean up.

"Go and play, dear," Mrs. Keeper said to Kaybee. "I'll clean up."

Kaybee kissed her mother on the cheek. "Thank you." She turned to us. "Would you like to go up to my room?"

"Sure," Gwen and I said.

It was a relief to get away from Kaybee's parents. I still couldn't believe how normal and boring they were. If there was a big secret about the strange way Kaybee behaved, her parents certainly didn't give us any clues.

As we climbed the wide staircase I asked Kaybee what she was going to be for Hallowe'en.

"What am I going to be?" She said. "Oooo, that's fun. I could be anything at all, couldn't I? Oooo. I know! I think I will be air."

"Air?" I said. "How can you dress up as air?"

"Oh!" Kaybee said. "You mean what *costume* will I wear. Foolie me. In that case, I think I will be fog. Yes, I will be fog."

I gave up.

We turned left at the top of the stairs, walked down a hallway, then entered Kaybee's room.

I was shocked for the third time. This was more like it!

Her room was *BLUE*! It was a huge room, and all of it was brilliant blue—the bed, dressing table, desk, chair, walls, everything.

Then Gwen gasped. "My gosh!" She was looking up.

I looked up, too. I couldn't believe my eyes. The ceiling looked like the sky on a clear night. Glittering white stars were painted all over the ceiling.

"Like it?" Kaybee said.

"It's—it's incredible!" Gwen said.

"Yeah," I said.

Then something came into the room. It was almost a dog but not quite. At least it was like no dog I'd ever seen. It was greyish-white. It had hundreds of thick strips of hair that hung down with clumps at the ends, like stretched-out pieces of chewing-gum. It looked like a gigantic mop with a pink tongue.

The thing sneezed.

"Come on, boy," Kaybee said. The thing wobbled into the room. "Jeff, Gwen, meet Sneeze. Say hello, Sneeze".

The thing sneezed again. I was about ready to bolt from the room, out of the window if I had to. Freaky!

"Be right back," Kaybee said. She vanished into the other room, then quickly returned with a blue rocking chair. When Sneeze saw the chair, he started thumping around all happylike. Kaybee placed it on the floor, and Sneeze immediately jumped up and sat in it.

"What kind of dog is that?" Gwen asked.

"Komondor," Kaybee said.

"Why does he sneeze so much?" I asked.

Kaybee giggled. "Poor Sneeze is allergic to himself."

The whole time we were in Kaybee's room, Sneeze sat there in the rocking chair, staring at us. And every time he sneezed, he rocked.

Then I noticed that over by the window was a huge telescope, pointing up at the sky. Beside that was a long table with maps and charts spread out all over it.

"This," Kaybee said, "is where I look up."

"You study the stars?" Gwen asked.

"Yes."

"Wow," I said, walking around in a circle, looking up at the ceiling, getting dizzy. "It looks real."

"It is," Kaybee said. "It is exact."

"What are these?" Gwen asked. She was over by the far wall, studying a picture that hung there.

I walked over. It was more of Kaybee's artwork, more weird planets with weird aliens.

"These are planets," Kaybee said proudly.

"Where do you get all your ideas for these?" Gwen asked.

"I look up," Kaybee said.

"You can't see all that from down here," I said, laughing. "Gwen means, how did you think up—"

"But I did see all these," Kaybee said.

My next question was: "Huh?"

Kaybee continued her wacky way. "Mummer and Dadder think these space pictures are space rubbish."

"Why?" Gwen asked.

Kaybee shrugged sadly.

"Will you tell us where you used to live?" I asked.

"It is hard to be specific about that. It was such a nowhere, do-nothing place." Kaybee said.

"Come on, Kaybee," Gwen said, "we're your friends. Tell us a little about yourself, will you? Jeff and I are dying to know."

"You would not believe me if I told you," Kaybee said. "And if you did believe me, you would not be my friends any longer."

"What's that mean?" Gwen was getting very angry.

Kaybee shrugged again.

"Okay, okay," Gwen said. "Forget it, just forget it."

"You are angry," Kaybee said.

Gwen shook her head. "No, I'm not."

"You are, you are. You are madder than the whirling firedogs of Wynaag."

"Cut...it...out!" Gwen screamed. "There are no whirling firedogs and there is no Wynaag!"

"There are!" Kaybee screamed back.

"We're trying to be your friends, can't you see that?" I'd never seen Gwen so mad. "Why do you have to talk to us like that? What's the matter with you? We...are...your...friends!"

I was caught in the crossfire, so I backed up against the wall, near the door, ready to bolt.

"If—If—If—" Kaybee said, "if you are my friends, why are you asking so many questions? I am *me!* I talk this way! I know what the firedogs look like—you don't! You are just making fun of me like everybody else. You think I am a weirding because I wear spaceish clothes. Because I cannot ride a bike. Because I do not sleep with a pillow..."

No pillow?

"...because I cannot bounce a ball and because earth music makes me throw up!"

Earth music?

"Kaybee," Gwen said, calmer now, "we don't care what your hobbies are. We're just trying to understand you."

"Why?" Kaybee said. "I do not try to understand the depths of you. I did not ask why you looked at me strangely when I told you to put your troubles in the trees. It is a nice saying. I like it. And I do not look at you strangely when you say weird things like 'Hiya' and 'Seeya' and 'Take it easy'. I don't even know what they mean!"

Gwen walked closer to Kaybee and put a hand on her shoulder. Kaybee twisted away. "Kaybee, listen. You don't really believe all that stuff about troubles in the trees and firedogs, I know you don't."

"It is *all* I believe!" Kaybee said. "I am not like you at all. I do not know of the things you know. You will *never* understand me! So you can *never* be my friends!"

And Kaybee started cyring.

Then Mr. and Mrs. Keeper came into the room.

"What's the matter in here?" asked Mr. Keeper.

"Oh, Kaybee," Mrs. Keeper said. She

hugged her strange daughter.

"I guess we'd better be going," Gwen said, and not soon enough for me. I was puzzled, baffled, confused—and scared out of my mind.

"See ya Kaybee," I said. "I mean, good-bye."

Kaybee didn't even look up.

"Kaybee," Gwen said, "we're sorry we upset you. We *are* trying to be your friends. Can't you try, too?"

Kaybee lifted her eyes to Gwen and nodded.

"Good," Gwen said. "Bye. Come over anytime, okay?"

Kaybee nodded.

We said thank-you and good-bye to Mr. and Mrs. Keeper and left the house. When we got to our bikes, my hands were shaking, my back was sweaty, and I couldn't hold it in any longer.

"Gwen. This is serious."

"I know."

"Gwen. I think I know Kaybee's secret."

"What?"

"Gwen, Kaybee's an alien."

ELEVEN

"*Alien!?* Really Jeffrey, this is no time for that. The answer to Kaybee's behaviour is somewhere in what we saw and heard in there. Maybe it's because of her parents, I don't know. There's more to it than meets the eye. And...Jeffrey, you're not listening, are you?"

"No. I'm telling you, I know I'm right. As soon as I thought of it, I knew I was right. When she started screaming, I *knew* I was right. Gwen, Kaybee is from outer space. Believe me. She has to be. There's no other reason for all that weirdness."

"Jeffrey—"

"Gwen! I can *prove* it!"

We wandered into the woods. Actually, we argued our way into the woods. We sat on a rock beside a brook and babbled. Gwen thought my imagination had run wild. She wasn't ready to believe that Kaybee was an alien, but she was willing to listen to my proof. I gave it to her.

"Sit back, Gwen, and listen to the evidence."

"This ought to be good."

"It is. Now. Right from the first time we met Kaybee, we thought there was something different about her. Her strange dresses. The nut-o way she talks. The goofy way she acts. You have to admit, Kaybee is not like anybody else."

"True. But it doesn't make her an alien J.M."

"Just wait, just wait." Gwen was laughing at me. She was sitting there smugly, waiting for me to make a fool of myself. "Now. Another thing is that Kaybee won't tell us anything about herself. Why? Why doesn't anyone else know anything about her? And why did our investigation turn up nothing? I'll tell you why. It's because there is nothing to find out. Kaybee has no past—no *Earth* past, anyway. She's keeping her frightening secrets to herself."

"Big deal, Jeffrey. So Kaybee's a private person, big deal."

"She's also from outer space. What about that speed-reading? What Earth kid can speed-read like that?"

"I have to admit that was impressive."

"You bet your nose it was. And on top of that, Kaybee knew nothing about geography. Why? Because she doesn't know anything about the planet Earth. Why? Because she's from *another* planet, that's why."

"Plenty of kids stink in geography."

"Yeah, but add that to the other stuff and it gets pretty creepy. Plus Kaybee doesn't even know how to ride a bike. She doesn't sleep with a pillow. She makes sandwiches inside out. And she said she hates Earth music. *Earth* music? And what about that dog of hers? If that dog's not from outer space, nothing is! Gwen, it all adds up to somebody who lives very, very far away."

"Jeffrey, this is crazy."

"Okay, okay. Now we get to some really good evidence. The letter. The letter in *code*. Why would anybody write a letter in code? I'll tell you why. Because it's a *secret* letter. She sure didn't want us to see it, did she? She sure didn't want to talk about it right? In fact, I'd say she was pretty darned scared. In fact, I think it was a letter to her home planet, asking them for news or maybe telling them how her mission on Earth was going."

"Oh, come on."

"*But!* But the letter wasn't as strange as her drawing in art class or the drawings on her bedroom wall."

"Yes, the drawings are strange, but—"

"You bet they are. They look real, too. A little *too* real. What did she call that planet in art class? Ooggeer? Maybe Ooggeer is her home planet. Maybe she has a firedog for a pet."

"And maybe she's just an original artist," Gwen said. "She loves those paintings, Jeffrey. Everytime she looks at them it looks like she's almost going to cry."

"Homesick! She's homesick! Remember

when we asked Kaybee if she'd ever run away from home? She got this really sad look hanging all over her face and said she ran away from home once but she didn't want to talk about it. Sure she didn't want to talk about it—her home is probably a billion light-years away! When she ran away from home, she came to Earth!"

Gwen shook her head. "Things like this just don't happen."

"Sure they do. They *are* happening. Kaybee's in love with space. She's got it painted on her ceiling, for crying out loud. Stars all over the place. She studies the stars every night."

"Plenty of people do."

"Yeah, but, Gwen, there's one thing that is the biggest piece of proof of all."

"What?"

"Her parents."

"Your're not going to tell me *they're* aliens, too!"

"Hey! I didn't think of that. Maybe they are. But why are they so different from Kaybee? Her father worked for the government, but they didn't tell us what he did. Maybe it's top secret! Maybe it has to do with Kaybee being from Ooggeer. And why won't they tell us where they used to live? I'm telling you, Gwen, Kaybee's parents have a big secret of their own, I know they do."

Gwen got to thinking. "I wonder why Mr. and Mrs. Keeper put up with Kaybee. They ignore her weirdness as if it doesn't exist."

"Maybe they're afraid of Kaybee. Maybe Kaybee has them under some powerful alien spell."

Gwen looked at me hard. "You're really making a jerk out of yourself J.M."

I shrugged. I felt that I had discovered the real truth behind Kaybee. It had to be true..I just wished I could convince Gwen, too.

We sat there a moment and watched the brook roll by. A bird sang, then flew away. A squirrel clattered up a tree. I swallowed.

"Gwen, there comes a time when you have to add up all the facts and get an answer. The answer is that Kaybee is an alien. I can't even think of a good reason why she *isn't* an alien. Can you?"

"Because things like this only happen in Slug Giants movies, J.M. Besides, Kaybee's nice."

"Come on, Gwen! Just because you like Kaybee doesn't mean she can't be an alien."

"I'm telling you, Jeffrey, you are wrong. And I'm not going to sit here and watch you get yourself into even more trouble. What are you going to do now?"

"What now? First I am going to tell Dave the news. I've discovered Kaybee's secret, Gwen! Our friends won't hate us anymore when we tell them this! Great, huh?"

"Not so great, J.M. They won't believe a word you say."

"Oh."

"If you insist on telling everyone that Kaybee

is from outer space, you'd better have some solid evidence, Jeffrey. So far all you have are guesses, zilch and zip."

"Yeah. Hmmmm. Evidence. Solid. Like photos or something. Like a spaceship or something. Like proof of her mission. Her mission! Gwen! Her mission! Kaybee must be on Earth for a reason! If she is an alien, there has to be a mission. A big mission. An important mission. A mission involving the whole school. Maybe the whole country."

"This is ridiculous!"

"Maybe the whole world! Global security is at stake here, Gwen. We owe it to our country to get solid proof. What if Mr. and Mrs. Keeper are the dangerous ones? Maybe they *are* aliens—I'm not ruling that out yet. Maybe they're on a secret mission for evil beings from another galaxy or a planet that's fighting with Ooggeer. Who knows? Or maybe they even work for foreign spies in our own government. Yeah, I need proof. Something I can take to the president—I just hope he's not involved, too. Something that'll show our creepy ex-friends that Jeff Moody has cracked the case of the century."

"I think you've cracked your skull," Gwen said. "Relax, J.M. Calm down. Get a grip on yourself. Think a minute, will you? What's going to happen when you find out you're wrong?"

"*If* I'm wrong, I lose my friends forever, I get

into a heap of trouble, and I'll probably be arrested and punished for fifty years. I know the stakes, Gwen. But if I'm right, I might be saving the world. There's only one way to find out. I have to go undercover, Gwen. I have to become...a spy."

TWELVE

Gwen told me and told me that I was going too far. I didn't listen. I wouldn't listen. I had to uncover Kaybee's mission. I had to warn the world.

The next morning, I got up an hour earlier.

I found my black turtleneck sweater and put it on. I slid into my black jeans. Black socks. Old, dirty trainers. I slipped on my denim jacket. Flipped on my dark blue baseball cap. The disc camera fitted perfectly into the right-hand pocket of my denim jacket. A small notebook and pen went into the other pocket. I dropped my pocketknife into the pocket of my jeans.

I was ready.

I went downstairs, wolfed down some cereal and orange juice, and headed the front door. The sun was low, but it was pretty bright out. It was then that I realized that black clothes only worked at night when it was dark and you could blend into the shadows. Who cared?

I headed out for Kaybee's house.

When I got there, I found the perfect tree and climbed it. Immediately my head began to whirl. Soon, though, the dizziness passed—as long as I didn't look down. I had a perfect view of Kaybee's house.

I scanned the windows. No lights. The Keepers were still sleepers. Good.

I began taking pictures.

Click. Click. Click. The clicking sounded like cannon blasts to me. Would it wake them up? No. They'd probably think it was crickets. Click. Click. Click.

I was a spy, and I had to think like one. I had to notice things that everyday people wouldn't notice. Little things. Tiny things. So I snapped pictures of everything I could see. A beetle. A bird. I even took a few pictures of the tree I was in, and one of me.

I climbed down. My legs were wobbly, but they soon stiffened up. The sun was getting brighter and higher all the time, so I had to hurry. I took shots of the grass as I walked to the right side of the house.

I crept all the way round the house taking pictures. A ladybird landed on my arm. I took its picture. It flew off. Shy.

I backed up, trying to shoot the entire back of the house, and stepped into the brook. A little brook ran down beside the Keeper's house, and I was now standing in it up to my ankles. I stepped out and took a few shots of the stupid brook. I moved round the house.

Squish. Squish. Squish.

My feet were floating in my trainers. I was afraid I'd wake somebody up. I tried to walk quietly as I finished up the photos.

Squish. Squish. Squish.

A light went on in the window above me. I didn't know whose room it was, and I didn't wait to find out. I stuffed my camera in my pocket, peeked round the front of the house, then ran.

Squish Squish Squish Squish Squish Squish Squish Squish Squish Squish Squish.

That night, I was back again to take some shots in the dark. I had to cut my mission short when I fell out of the tree and said, "Whoa!"

So far I had nothing. But my spying had only just begun. The next morning and night I took some more shots of the Keepers' house, and in the morning after that, I began Phase Two.

For the next two days I followed Kaybee the alien everywhere.

At the bus stop I noticed how she tied her shoe. I took notes. I wrote down what she wore, what she said on the bus, who she talked to. In class I wrote down what questions she knew and which ones she didn't know. Everything went into my notebook. What she ate at lunch and how many times she went to the girls' room. I tried to get her exact words when she said one of her weird sayings. By the end of the day, my notebook was filled. When Gwen and I got off the bus to go home, Kaybee got off with us.

"Hello, Jeffrey, Gwen," Kaybee said.

"Hi, Kaybee," Gwen said.

"Well, what do you know," I said. "Kaybee. Haven't seen you in a while."

"You've seen me all day, Jeffrey. We go to school together."

"True. True."

"I am walking you home. I have something to say."

She'd seen me following her, I knew it. How can I talk my way out of this one? I shrugged and said, "Okay."

"Jeffrey," Kaybee said, "are you still my friend?"

"Of course, silly."

"But you are so sad and jumpy all the time, like the Bizzi Beans of the planet Vid."

Whew! I guess she didn't notice me all day. "Nerves," I said.

"Hot herbal tea," she said. "Try some Red Zinger."

"I sure will, Kaybee," I said. "Thanks."

Soon Kaybee left and Gwen gave me a lecture.

"Jeffrey, you are carrying this thing too far. Everybody in the whole world saw you following Kaybee today."

"Everybody except Kaybee."

"Doesn't matter. You looked like a jerk. Hiding in doorways, peeking round corners, taking notes. What have you found out?"

I hung my head. "Nothing new. She didn't

do anything alien. I don't even know what I'm looking for."

"Give it up, J.M. You'll never find any proof this way."

"I have to! I want my friends back, Gwen. They keep bugging me for the big secret I said I had. I have to come up with something, or they'll hate me even more. Besides, Gwen, you're forgetting that there's an alien girl in our school. It's up to me to prove it, to tell the government, to warn the world."

"What's your next step?"

"Next comes Phase Three."

"Phase Three? What's that?"

"Kaybee's parents."

"Jeffrey, you're not really going to spy on her parents!"

I nodded. "You bet I am. More and more I'm sure that they're the key. They're going to leave clues, Gwen, and I'm going to be there to pick them up."

"Jeffrey…"

"See you in a couple of days."

"A couple of…Jeff!"

I skipped school the next day.

I was a boy obsessed. Plus, I was a spy. Nothing stops a spy from succeeding at his mission.

I hid in the bushes outside the Keepers' house until Kaybee left for school. Then I waited a little more. Today I was going to follow the Keepers everywhere they went. But what if they left separately? I couldn't follow two people at the same time. What then? Luckily I didn't have to worry about that today. When they finally came out, they came out together. They got in their car together and drove off together. I hopped on my bike and rode my brains out.

If they were driving far away, I'd never keep up. But they weren't. They drove to the centre of town and parked. Then they walked around.

Great. Luck was with me today. I'd tail them all day, find out where these shady people went, take pictures, write notes, and be there if they met a government agent or maybe another alien. But I had to be careful. The Keepers were hiding an alien girl, and if they caught me and found out I knew the truth, it would be curtains.

I hid behind a fat lady and followed them down the pavement.

They bought a screwdriver at the ironmongers. Mrs. Keeper had her hair done at the hairdresser. They browsed in the pet shop. They bought two chickens at the butcher's. They bought Hallowe'en toffee at the sweetshop.

Frankly, I was getting bored. Was spying always this dull?

They went into the bakery. I decided to wait outside in a doorway. I was bent over, shaking the dirt out of the turn ups of my jeans when I saw them walking right towards me! I'd been spotted! They were coming to ask me what I was doing here, and if I didn't have the right answer—oops! A knife in the gut. A bullet to the heart. One of those rope things around my neck.

I did the only thing I could do. I turned round and faced the doorway, making believe I was about to go inside. I tried the doorknob. Locked. I made believe I was looking for my keys in my pocket. I peeked back. They were a few metres away. I was sweating like ice cubes in a frying pan.

They stopped right behind me, talking.

"Shall we kill them tonight?" Mrs. Keeper said.

Kill them!? Kill who?

"No, no," Mr. Keeper said. "Not tonight. Not so soon. Maybe tomorrow."

Murderers! They're murderers! Who are they going to kill? Me and Gwen?

"Oh, come on, honey. Let's knock them off tonight. Right after dinner. We love to do that, you know we do."

They were going to kill us *tonight!*

Mr. Keeper laughed. "Oh, all right. We'll knock them off after dinner."

I had to tell Gwen! We had to hide! Get away! But I couldn't do anything until the Keepers left.

"Good! I'm excited. You think they'll still be fresh?"

"Of course they will. Apple turnovers don't

go stale that quickly. Besides, we'll knock them off before they have a chance to go stale."

And Mr. and Mrs. Keeper walked off.

I slid down the door and sat on the stop. All they were going to kill tonight were two apple turnovers. I'd almost had a heart attack for nothing.

I looked at my watch. School was almost over. I found out nothing today. Time to go home.

I should never have gone home.

THIRTEEN

As soon as I stepped through the front door, Mum came flying down the stairs from her attic art studio. Her face was red, her eyes wide, and her hands were fists. She was mad. I backed up against the wall and tried to get flat. I felt sure she was going to start punching me and never stop.

Mum stamped up to me, puffing hard, grabbed my elbow, and shook my arm. "Where were you today? Answer me! I want an answer right now!"

"I—"

"What's the matter with you, Jeff? Have you suddenly turned into a criminal? A juvenile delinquent? I thought you had more brains than this." She shook my arm some more. "Well? Where were you?"

"I—"

"Ooo, you just wait until your father comes home. You just wait! Where *were* you!"

"Mum, I—"

"The school called, Jeffrey, the *school*! Your teacher! You weren't there today, they said. You skipped school! Why? *Why?*"

I was scared. If I said anything now, I was afraid she'd ground me for life. I didn't dare to think about what Dad would do.

"Upstairs. Get upstairs until your father comes home. Don't do anything. Just sit up there and come down when you're called. Move!"

I moved, and I moved fast. I ran into my room and sat on the bed. My heart was leaping around inside my chest. My palms were sweaty. Even my feet throbbed. I really did it this time. What's wrong with me? What made me think I could get away with skipping school? I rested there until my body got back to almost normal.

It all might be worth it, though, I thought. There was an alien girl in town. The stakes were high. If I didn't get to the bottom of it, who would? But what now? I was caught, and if I was punished, I might not be able to stop Kaybee's mission, whatever that was. Should I tell Mum and Dad the truth? Never. I just couldn't. I still had no proof, and they'd never believe me. I'd have to take the punishment like any spy would. I'd have to survive the questions, the torture—but I wouldn't talk!

Then I heard Dad come through the front door. Right away Mum started telling him about how my teacher called because I'd skipped school. Then Dad called me down.

I shuffled down the stairs and into the living room. I didn't feel like a secret agent anymore.

I felt like a scared little boy who was about to get punished for the rest of his life.

Dad pointed to the sofa and I sat down. I felt very small. He just stared at me for a moment with his hands on his hips, shaking his head. Then he held up his left hand, and with his right forefinger he touched fingers on his left hand.

"You didn't do your history homework. Your maths homework. Your biology homework. No homework all week. You skipped school today to do who knows what. You were caught. Now you're going to be punished." He'd run out of fingers and put his hands back on his hips. "First I want to know why. Then I want to know where you went."

I decided to lie. I decided the truth would be much worse because the truth sounded like an even bigger lie.

"I don't know," I said.

"What do you mean you don't know?" Mum said.

"Jeff," Dad said, "why didn't you do your homework all week?"

I shrugged. "I don't know. I didn't feel like it."

"Okay, okay," Mum said. "Sometimes kids just don't feel like doing any homework. That's no excuse, but it happens. So why did you skip school today? Where did you go?"

"The pictures."

"The *pictures!*" Mum shrieked.

"I want a *reason*, Jeff," Dad said. "You've

103

never done anything like this before. Why? Why?"

"I don't know, Dad. School was really getting to me. I'm really sorry I did it, though. It was stupid."

Maybe it was because I looked so scared. Maybe it's because I apologized. Or maybe Dad decided to go easy on me because it was the first time in a long time that I'd done something really horrible. I don't know, but they didn't ask me for any more reasons. Dad and Mum talked for a minute, then Mum let Dad announce my punishment.

"You have to make up all your homework, starting right now. You have to wash and dry all the dishes for a month. You'll get no allowance. And for one month you can play with your friends only one day a week, and it's right home after school every day."

Dinner was silent. Joey kept asking, "What's wrong, what's wrong?" But nobody told him what I'd done. I think he began to feel *he'd* done something wrong.

After dinner I went upstairs to my room. I dived for my bed, trying to do one complete twist in midair before I landed. I didn't make it.

I had already done all my homework, I'd just been too busy tailing Kaybee to turn it in, so I stretched out on my bed and did some heavy thinking.

First I thought about Gwen. She's a great friend, she really is. Smart, too. Then I thought about my other friends. Dave, Lou, Mack, even Tandy. All of them. Each of them is fun to hang around with. I felt kind of solid thinking about them, knowing that they were out there, my buddies. I just wished they didn't hate me right now.

Then I got to thinking about my room, my house, my street, and my whole neighbourhood. I've lived here all my life. My neighbourhood is pretty average, I suppose, but I know it like I know a friend. I know every bump in the road and every path through the woods. I know all the dogs and cats. I know where to catch frogs and which kids scream the loudest when you drop one down their shirts.

But out there in the house on the hill was somebody I didn't know at all. Someone I knew only because of the weird things she did. I was thinking about Kaybee. Kaybee, the girl from outer space. It was incredible. It was fantastic. It was horrifying. What was she up to? And why was she up to it in my neighbourhood? I thought over the facts.

Fact: Kaybee's an alien. Fact: Her father works for the government, and no one knows where the Keepers came from, and the Keepers aren't talking. Fact: Kaybee must have some kind of mission. Fact: If I can find out what it is, I stop her mission, get back all my friends, and get my life back to normal. Fact: I was beginning to suspect that someone was out to stop me.

I thought it was strange that just when I was starting to spy on Kaybee and her parents, my teacher decided to call my folks. That was the scary part. Usually the principal calls when a kid doesn't show up. So why did Mrs. Binker call?

Could Mrs. Binker be in on the whole thing? Did the Keepers see me and call the school? Maybe the entire school was in on it! Maybe the school was out to stop me from revealing that Kaybee was from outer space!

I sat up. Now I was *really* scared. Had I discovered a massive conspiracy? I knew one thing: I had to be careful. From now on I could be in danger.

Soon I yawned. I stopped thinking. I rose and locked all the windows. I undressed and settled between the sheets. Silence closed around me like a hundred pairs of earmuffs. A tree clawed at my window. I slept like a log.

The next morning, while we were waiting for class to start, I told Gwen what I thought.

"Ridiculous," she said. "Mrs. Binker, a spy for the government, covering up for a weird alien girl? Ridiculous."

"It could happen, Gwen. A lot of strange things have been going on."

"True, Jeffrey, but most of them have been going on in your head. Okay, I'll admit that there is a mystery. I'll admit that I am curious about why Kaybee does all the things she does, too. But, Jeffrey, if your not careful, you are going to get into a whole bunch of trouble."

"Yeah, I know. I'm already in trouble."

Just then, Kaybee came into the classroom. "Good morning, Jeffrey. Hi, Gwen. We missed you in school yesterday, Jeffrey. There was quite a void at your desk that was really quite sad to look at. I hope that from now on you will make us all happy and be in school every day."

Was that a threat? Did she know I was staking out her house and following her and her parents around? Right then I decided to spy on Kaybee all day. I decided to keep an eye on crafty Mrs. Binker, too.

At lunchtime I went out to my locker in the hall to get my spy notebook. I'd put everything into that notebook, all the observations and evidence I had. If something happened to me, the notebook would remain as solid proof that I had been done in by an alien plot.

As I spun the combination on my locker, Dave walked up and started opening the locker next to mine.

"Say there, strange one," Dave said. "Haven't seen much of you lately."

"Hi, Dave."

"You know, Jeff, we're all still waiting for that big secret of yours. You remember, don't you? The big secret about Kaybee Keeper that only you know."

"Yeah, yeah."

"Ha. You don't have any secret and you know it."

"I do, too! And I'm not telling you until I'm

good and ready."

I flung open my locker door. I dug under books and books for my notebook. Then I dug some more.

The notebook was gone.

"Jeff, are you okay?" Dave said, grabbing my arm as I fell back against the lockers. "You look like you've seen a ghost."

The notebook was *gone!* I couldn't believe it. It was stolen right out of my locker. Stolen by who? It had to be Kaybee or someone else who was in on the conspiracy. I started to get the shakes.

"Jeff?" Dave was leaning over and looking hard into my face.

"Dave, I have to tell you something. I have to tell somebody before it's too late."

"Before what's too late?"

"It's the secret. Kaybee's secret. It's dangerous. Very dangerous."

"Huh?"

I grabbed the front of Dave's shirt. "Promise you won't tell anyone else. It has to stay a secret, but if anything happens to me, I want you to know. Promise."

"Yeah, sure, okay, I promise. What is it?"

I gulped. "This is going to be hard to believe, Dave, but trust me, okay? It's true. All the facts were in a notebook here in my locker. Now somebody's stolen the notebook. It's trouble, Dave, big trouble."

"What's the secret?"

I looked left. I looked right. I looked at Dave. I whispered. "Kaybee is not just some weird girl, Dave. She's from outer space. She's an alien, Dave, on some kind of mission. We have to stop her."

Dave said, *"Ffft."* Then he said, *"Hup,"*. Then he said, "Ha. Haha. Haha-heee. Yah-ha-hahahahahaha."

"It's true!" I screamed.

"This is your big secret? Yah-hahafff. You're more wacko than she is!" And Dave closed his locker and laughed his way down the hall.

FOURTEEN

It was Saturday morning now, Hallowe'en. I still had no idea who took my notebook.

After breakfast I asked if today could be my one-day play day—that way, I could go out trick-or-treating tonight. Mum and Dad said okay. I gave Gwen a call.

"Gwen? Jeff."

"Hi, J.M. Any new leads on your notebook?"

"No."

"Anything new on the alien conspiracy theory?"

I knew she was making fun of me. "Only that I've got a strong feeling that time is running out fast."

"Why?"

"Haven't you noticed? Something's happened to Kaybee. She's quiet now."

"Yes, I have noticed. She's not as weird as she was, is she? Maybe she's trying to fit in."

"Maybe her mission is over and she's ready to go back to her own planet."

"Maybe, maybe, maybe. Jeff, be realistic."

"I'm trying, Gwen."

"Good. So why'd you call me?"

"Oh. Wanna go to the Zoo?"

"You're on. See you there in half an hour."

I felt better already. It there's one place on earth where I can forget my troubles, it's the Zoo.

She hung up. I hung up. I grabbed my black jacket with orange stripes on the sleeves and a picture of a mean bumblebee on the back above bright orange letters that said **BUG OFF!** I bounced over to my money box, filled my pockets, lost my balance running down the stairs and slammed the front door, yelled to whoever could hear me that I was going out and I'd be back for supper, Mum yelled okay, Dad yelled okay, I left.

I rushed outside and hopped onto my trusty old J.C. Penney dirt bike. It's black, beat-up, with bald tyres. Forty-seven of my favourite stickers are stuck all over it. It's really me. I'll keep it until it falls apart. I popped a wheelie before roaring up my street, Blackwell Court. Just past Mr. Crean's house I shot off the street and hit the field, riding hard. When I was nearly on Route 99, I slammed on the brakes and did a sideways skid onto the shoulder and stopped with an impressive whoosh of dust. I looked both ways twice, then zagged across the road, zigged over to Cole Street, burned rubber past the Launderette and the supermarket as I made loud gear-shifting sounds, then leaned hard into a right turn that whizzed me to a screeching halt in front of a small red building called Electronic Zoo, the best video game arcade around.

Two seconds later Gwen rolled up beside me on her white trail bike.

I love the Zoo. I love all the games. I love the crowd of screaming kids and adults who act like kids. I love the *breeeep, eeeoorrk,* and *bee-doo-bee-doo-bee-doo* sounds. Like I said, I love the Zoo.

"I love the Zoo," Gwen said.

"Not me," I said, and bolted ahead to beat her to the entrance, my change jingling happily in my pocket.

We went in.

Today the Zoo was packed. Everyone was there. Men, women, mothers, fathers, grandfathers, boys, girls, little kids, big kids, fat kids, skinny kids, you name it. Doesn't matter who you are, everybody has fun at the Zoo. And right now they were twisting, grunting, screaming, bending, and ooing as the lights of green, orange, red, blue, white, and yellow were shooting, blinking, exploding, swirling, crashing, and fizzing, while the loud electronic machines made those *zing, biong, weet, greep, jaaag, oos-oos-oooz,* and *quarrrrrivit* sounds I mentioned before. What a place.

Against the left wall I saw my ex-teacher, mean Mrs. Burns, shout loudly and kick a machine.

"Well, if it isn't star boy."

I looked towards the voice. It was Dave. Other kids I knew were there, too, and they were looking at me and laughing. I guessed Dave told everybody that I thought Kaybee was an alien. Terrific.

"Shut up, Dave," I said. And I shoved my way to the other side of the room.

Gwen followed me. "Jeff, you didn't tell Dave, did you?"

"Yeah."

"Big mistake, J.M. Now everybody will know. Now they'll all be laughing at you and making fun of you and—"

"I know, I know."

I crammed a coin into a game before I even knew which game it was. I played it for about thirty seconds and lost. Then I felt somebody looking over my shoulder. I turned around.

"Hi, freak."

It was Pinky Nickle.

"Beat it, huh?"

"Why, Jeffrey Moody, I thought you'd be happy to see me."

"You thought wrong. I'm never happy to see you."

She smiled at me and giggled. "Jeffrey, did you know I was psychic?"

"I know you're a jerk."

"Ha. Ha. Wait, wait, something is coming in now. Unnnn. Yes, it's very clear now. You have ...lost something. It's...it's a notebook."

"You stole it!"

"Wrong, wrong, wrong. I found it. You left it under your desk in class."

"Give it to me."

"Oh, I can't do that, Jeffrey. I've not finished reading it yet. It's very entertaining."

I felt like hitting her. But before I could, I heard a high voice float through the Zoo.

"Mipping Mippers! I thought I'd never find you!"

It was Kaybee Keeper. She slid through the crowd and up to me and Pinky. Gwen came over too.

"Hi, Kaybee," Gwen said.

"Hello!" Kaybee yelled. "Ooshy gracious, I am happier than a hoprock on Fymore. I hope you two aren't mad at me?"

"Mad at you?" I said.

"Goodness, yes. I haven't met you at your house in time uncounted! Ahh, Jeffrey and Gwen. My two bestest of friends on Earth. Let's do something together as a threesome today."

"Hi, Kaybee," Pinky said. "Funny you should show up. We were just talking about you."

"No, we weren't," I said. My stomach began to feel very heavy.

"Of course, we were, Jeffrey. Don't lie to Kaybee."

"Jeffrey would never lie to me," Kaybee said.

Pinky smiled. "No, of course not. Jeff would

never lie. But he might just not tell you things on purpose."

Just then Dave ambled over with a couple of other kids. He must not have seen Kaybee at first, because he said, "Hey, Jeff, tell us. What planet did you say Kaybee was from?"

Everybody laughed. Then Dave saw Kaybee and said, "Whoops."

Kaybee frowned and looked puzzled.

"Knock it off, Dave," I said.

"Funny you should ask," Pinky said. "Let's look it up." She held out her hand, and one of her friends handed her my notebook. I tried to grab it but missed. "Let's see now," Pinky said, flipping throught the notebook. "Here it is. Ooggeer. Kaybee is from the planet Ooggeer."

Kaybee's head was whipping back and forth from me to Pinky to Dave to Gwen to everybody. "What is that book? Is that your book, Jeffrey? Why am I in your book?"

"Because the book's all about you," Pinky said. "See, Jeffrey has been spying on you, Kaybee. Know why?"

"No."

"Because he thinks you are an alien from outer space."

Kaybee's face turned bright red. "Even if I was a six-legged Tumble-Toad, Jeffrey would never make fun of me in writing or in word! He is my *friend!*"

Pinky held my notebook out to Kaybee. "Here, look for yourself."

I snatched the notebook. "I'm not making fun of you, Kaybee. We told you Pinky was a creep, but you didn't believe us."

Pinky turned to Dave. "Tell Kaybee what Jeff said to you, Dave."

Dave looked scared. "Uh, it was nothing. He didn't mean anything. He was joking around, that's all."

"But what did he say?"

"You must tell the truth, David," Kaybee said. "Lies do not keep company with friends."

Dave sighed heavily. "He said you were an alien on a secret mission on Earth."

Gwen put a hand on Kaybee's shoulder. "Jeff was only fooling, Kaybee."

"Yes, he was!" Kaybee said. "And you, Gwendolyn Sharp, let him do it!" She turned to me. "You have been making fun of me up and down and behind my back! Just like everybody else! I didn't think that my alien and otherworld interests made any difference to you. I thought you were my friend, to like me and stick by me no matter what anyone did or said. And I was your friend too, Jeffrey Moody. You had lunch at my house!"

Kaybee was freaking out.

"I *am* your friend," I said. "Don't listen to them, Kaybee. I was only trying to show them that you're not craz—uh, I mean..."

"You think I am crazy!" Kaybee yelped.

"No, I—" I really did it now.

And Pinky made it worse. "Sure Jeff thinks

you're crazy, Kaybee. Why else would he write all this weird stuff about you and show it to everybody? You might as well tell us the truth, Kaybee. Jeff and all of us are dying to know. Are you crazy? Or are you really an alien?"

"Shut up, Pinky!" I screamed.

"Kaybee?" Pinky said. "If you're crazy, Kaybee, you'd better go and get help fast. But if you're an alien, maybe you should just go home to your own crazy planet!"

Pinky and her gang burst out laughing. So did all the kids who gathered round to watch. The Zoo had become a zoo.

Kaybee started to cry. She lifted her head and glared at Pinky with sheer hate. Then she turned to me with a new wave of tears puring down her cheeks. "Oh, Jeffrey. You hated me all along. I ...You...I really thought..."

Kaybee looked down at the notebook in my hand, then she looked up to me one more time. Her face seemed to shrink, it all scrunched together and she let loose a horrible sob and raced out of the Zoo, banging back and forth between the people like a pinball.

I just stood there like a zombie. I felt like a blob of slime.

"Pinky," I said, "someday you'll be sorry for this. I'll make sure of it."

"Big talk from a guy who loves nutcakes," she said.

"Do you know what you've just done?" Gwen said to Pinky and Dave. "You've just broken that girl's heart. What's the matter with you jerks? Don't you think Kaybee has feelings?"

"Aw, she's a creep," Pinky said.

"Maybe she is," Dave said, "but I feel like one, too. Sorry, Jeff."

"You should say that to Kaybee," Gwen said.

Dave nodded and wandered off with his friends. Pinky smirked and left.

"See what your stupid spying has done now?" Gwen said to me.

I nodded. "Yeah, I do see. I feel horrible that Kaybee's upset. I know it's my fault, too. But I'm telling you, Gwen, right now, out there somewhere, is one mad alien girl."

"Jeffrey—"

"She's so mad, the whole Earth could be at stake!"

"Stop it!"

"Gwen, Kaybee didn't run off now because I think she's an alien—she almost admitted she was. No. She ran off because she thought I was her friend and I was making fun of her. She trusted me."

"It doesn't matter," Gwen said. "Now she hates you and she feels she hasn't got a friend in the world. She probably blames you for wrecking her whole life right now. I hope you're happy."

"No, I'm not happy. I'm scared. She not only hates me, Gwen, but she knows that I know she's on a secret mission. She knows that my spying found out that she's up to something. She's going to get me, Gwen. I know it. She's going to destroy me before I can talk. Unless I can find her first."

FIFTEEN

It was seven-thirty Hallowe'en night. Outside, a light, misty rain was falling, and the full moon looked like the foggy face of the Wizard of Oz. Inside, I had just finished helping Dad with the dishes.

Gwen was due over in half an hour. We had no plan, but we knew we'd have to find Kaybee. We thought having our costumes on would help—by pretending to trick-or-treat, we could get in anywhere. Plus, I didn't want Kaybee to recognize me and zap me before I apologized and explained. Now it was time for me to get into my costume.

Joey was in his Dracula costume. He looked more like a little bat than a master vampire. His plastic fangs were too big for his mouth and they kept falling out.

"I'd gobba bide your neck!" Joey said. He waved his black cape, opened his mouth, then dived to the floor for his teeth.

Mum was taking off her coat. She had just come back from taking Joey trick-or-treating—Dad had a slight cold and Mum wouldn't let him go. Igor had gone with them. Igor wore a bright red cape. He was Krypto the Superdog. He kept running circles, nipping and barking at the cape.

As Joey attacked his bag of goodies, I headed up the stairs.

"Putting on your costume now?" Dad asked.

"Yup," I said.

"Cab I watz?" Joey asked.

"Nope."

"Well, hurry it up," Mum said. "We're dying to see it!"

"Dying?" Joey said. He leaped to bite Mum's throat, but he was too short.

Half an hour later I left my room and started down the stairs.

Clump. Clump. Clump.

I heard Mum from the living room: "What's that thumping sound?"

"Beats me," Dad said. "But it's shaking the china."

Clump. Clump. Clump. Clump.

Igor saw me and started barking.

Joey ran up, gawked at me, and lost his fangs.

Mum and Dad appeared from the living room. Mum said "Eek!"

Dad looked me up and down and shook his head.

"*That's* my son?" Mum said.

"He must be," Dad said, "he looks just like you."

"Oh!" Mum said, whacking Dad on the arm.

I was Frankenstein's monster.

For my head I'd taken the brim off an old baseball cap and sewed a thick, square piece of cardboard on top of the cap. I covered the cardboard with fake hair. Green makeup covered my face, except for the area round my eyes, which was black. I'd drawn a purple scar around my forehead. Two plastic bolts were glued onto each side of my neck with spirit gum. I sewed balled-up towels into the shoulders of one of Dad's old sport coats to make me look huge and broad. My trousers were an old pair that I'd cut off raggedly round the bottom. But the shoes were the best part.

"What makes you thunk like that?" Mum asked.

"Horseshoes," I said. "I nailed horseshoes to the bottom of these old work boots. Sounds like I'm really heavy, huh?"

"Hey!" Joey screamed. "Your wrists are bleeding."

"Stitches," I said. "Comes from sewing my hands on. It's lipstick. Neat, huh?"

The doorbell rang. It was Gwen.

Gwen was a fairy princess in a long, golden wig, and she looked like a jerk. Her glasses didn't help, either.

"Frankenstein's monster," she said. "Cute. Hold it a second."

A second late I was standing at the bottom of the stairs facing Gwen, who was one step up trying to adjust my flattop wig.

She leaned closer and whispered, "I took a ride past Kaybee's on the way over. I didn't see her."

"I called."

"You did?"

"Yeah. I pretended I was Dave. Her parents said she wasn't home yet. I was going to apologize to her, just to keep her on my side you know? But I'm scared, Gwen. She could be anywhere. Plotting against me. Maybe getting a whole army of aliens. Wish I knew where she was."

"Jeffrey, please drop this alien fantasy, will you? I just hope she's okay."

The 'phone rang from round the corner in the living room. Mum answered it, and Gwen and I leaned closer to listen.

"Hello? ...oh, hello, Mr. Keeper.. Kaybee hasn't come home for dinner?...No, no, she hasn't been over here...Well, if you're that worried, maybe we can help find her...Sure you can come over to talk, we'd love to see you. Does Kaybee have our phone number in case she comes home while you're here?...Good, good, see you soon." Mum hung up and yelled to Dad that the Keepers were coming over.

"Something is going on," I said. "Something bad. I don't trust the Keepers one bit."

Gwen sat beside me on the stairs. "Wonder where she went."

"Probably back to her own planet to get

reinforcements!"

"Don't be ridiculous."

Mum came round the corner with a worried look on her face. "Oh, here you are. Have either of you seen Kaybee today?"

"No," I said.

Gwen and I looked at each other. Then Gwen blabbed. She told Mum everything that happened at the Zoo.

"I'm sure she'll be home soon," Dad said.

"We're not so certain," said Mr. Keeper. "This isn't the first time this has happened."

"No?" Mum said.

"We'd better tell you the whole story," said Mrs. Keeper. "We have to tell someone because, frankly, we just don't know what to do anymore. You see, Kaybee is adopted. We adopted her when she was just a baby. Through the years we gave her just about anything she wanted. Everything was fine until Kaybee found out she was adopted. She found some papers we had put away. That's when her problems began. That's when she changed. She'd always had a problem getting along with other children, but then her problems got worse. She started showing off just to shock people. She insisted on learning speed-reading to impress everybody. She joined a strange club called the Code Club—they write to each other in code. She makes up the wildest stories, and her fascination with outer space always gets her into trouble."

I leaned close to Gwen. "Gwen, did you hear that? I wonder—"

Gwen held a finger to her lips and said, "Shh, you dummy."

"Once," said Mr. Keeper, "Kaybee even told a teacher that she was a princess from another planet. Can you imagine? No matter what the teacher said, Kaybee swore it was true. She ended up in the principal's office, and the kids in school never stopped making fun of her. She's always trying too hard to get attention."

"So, anyway," Mrs. Keeper continued, "we blame ourselves. We had actually fooled ourselves into thinking that we were her real parents. We never thought about what to do when Kaybee found out we weren't. Now it might be too late."

"Don't be so hard on yourselves," Dad said. "Anybody would feel the way you do."

"I know, I know," Mrs. Keeper said, "but that still leaves us with Kaybee's problem. As I said, this isn't the first time she's run away."

"The first time she ran away," Mr. Keeper said, "was soon after she found out she was adopted. Between not being liked by the other kids and suddenly finding out her parents weren't her real parents."

"Alone?" Mum said.

"Yes," said Mr. Keeper. "She took a train and disappeared. She only went as far as the next stop before she got scared and came home. But by that time, we were out of our minds with worry and had already called the police. When the news broke out all over town and in her school, it was so upsetting to Kaybee and to us that we were pleased when I retired and we had the opportunity to move away and come here to start over. We hoped Kaybee would be happier here, but it hasn't worked out. She still insists on wearing those outrageous clothes. And she still makes up awful stories. Both of us are afraid to tell her not to wear those clothes. We're afraid she'll try to run away again. We were hoping that Kaybee would grow out of her problems."

"I'm sorry," Mum said. "What now?"

"We don't know what to do," Mrs. Keeper said. "We checked the railway station on our way over here, but she wasn't there. We don't want to call the police yet. After what happened last time, we just can't. We want to give Kaybee a chance to come home on her own, to fit in here. I just hope she comes home soon."

I felt rotten from head to toe. Poor Kaybee. I thought she was an alien for just wanting to be friends with me! Some friend I am!

Gwen grabbed my arm, and we went back up to my room and closed the door.

I knew Gwen was going to say. She was mad, and even though she was dressed up like a fairy princess, I didn't even think about laughing.

"You jerk!" she said. "Kaybee an alien—ha! She's a sad girl with big problems, and you just made her problems worse! You and your imagination! And I almost believed you!"

"Yeah, but, if Pinky didn't—"

"Forget Pinky! She's a low-down bully and always will be. If it wasn't for you and your spying and your notebook and your crazy theories, none of this would have happened."

Gwen was right. I fell into the beanbag chair in the corner. I looked down at my Frankenstein feet. I felt like bawling and screaming and eating the carpet. Kaybee had been showing off, making it all up! It was all my fault, I wrecked her life, and I felt like throwing up.

"Well, Jeffrey, what do we intend to do about this?"

"We have to do something before they decide to call the cops. I have to let Kaybee know I like her. I have to tell her I'm sorry. And I have to tell her that she's not the weird one—I *am!* But, Gwen, where is she?"

SIXTEEN

About half and hour later, we heard the Keepers leave. They said they wanted to go back in case Kaybee came home. They were pretty upset. If Kaybee didn't show up soon, they said they'd have to call the police.

I was pacing the room, making loud thumping noises with each step of my Frankenstein work boots. Gwen sat on my bed twirling her magic wand.

"Kaybee could be anywhere," I said. "A film, a shop, anywhere. She might even be in the basement of her own house."

Gwen shook her head. Her long blond wig-curls whipped around her face. "I don't think Kaybee is hiding, J.M. Last time she didn't hide, she ran away. I think she ran away this time, too."

"Then she could be in another state by now."

"Maybe. Maybe not. We won't find out until we look."

"Yeah. So what would you do if you ran away? Hitchhike? Hop a bus? Catch a train?"

"I don't think Kaybee would hitchhike, especially after dark," Gwen said. "There is no bus station in town, only a stop on the corner. If she doesn't want to be found, she wouldn't just stand out on an open corner. That leaves the railway station. But the Keepers already checked there and didn't find her."

"What if Kaybee wandered around for a while first?" I said. "What if she didn't decide to go to the railway station until now? What if, what if, what if! Face it, Gwen, we don't have a chance of finding her. But we have to! What do we do!"

"Easy J.M."

I gritted my teeth. The thought of Kaybee out there alone, probably crying and in danger, was tearing my guts. All this time I had been crazy to prove that Kaybee was from outer space. Well, now I was even crazier to find her.

"I can't just sit around here, Gwen. Let's get out there and find her! I know we can do it!"

"That's the spirit! Let's get organized."

"Yeah, we'll organize, that's what we'll do," I said. "We'll ride through town, check out Goggle's, the Zoo, other places, then head towards the railway station."

"Great!"

"Let's go!"

We raced out of the room and rushed downstairs. We tramped through the living room and into the kitchen, where Mum and Dad were having coffee.

"Mum, Dad," I said, "Gwen and I are going out trick-or-treating now."

"No, you're not," Dad said.

"Huh?" I said.

"Look outside," Mum said. "It's raining cats and dogs. You're not going out in that."

"But we have to!" I said. "We want to look for Kaybee."

"You'll never find her in that rain, Jeff," Dad said.

"We'll take umbrellas."

"No argument," Mum said. "You're not going out and that's that. Sorry, but that's the law until the rain stops."

I knew there was no sense in fighting. They always win. Gwen and I wandered through the living room, but I stopped her at the foot of the stairs.

"I'm going out," I said.

"How? You heard your parents."

"I don't care. I'm going anyway. Who knows what could happen to Kaybee. I have to find her, Gwen. I have to. You coming?"

Gwen smiled. "I'm right behind you, bucko."

I walked to the front door, opened it, let Gwen through first, followed her out, then closed the door behind us. Through the closed door I heard Dad yell, "Jeff! You get back in here!"

We took off.

SEVENTEEN

The fairy princess and Frankenstein's monster ran to their bikes, hopped on, and raced into the night. I didn't look back when I heard Dad screaming at me from the from porch. It was too late to turn back now.

Outside, the first thing I noticed was the heavy fog. It made it hard to see more than ten metres ahead. It was raining all right, but not cats and dogs. More like butterflies and gnats. None of that mattered, anyway. I would have looked for Kaybee that night if it was raining drawing pins.

As we roared along, the green makeup on my face started to run, and my flattop wig was getting heavy. I wiped my face with my sleeve. Gwen was soggy, too. Her big white dress looked like a wet dog. She stopped once to stuff her dress into the top of the jeans she wore underneath. We hit the streets again.

On the way to town we passed a few ghouls, ghosts, and robots, all with umbrellas, and all looking dripping wet. Some kids will do anything for free sweets. They stopped to look and point as we zoomed by and disappeared into the foggy night.

"Boy, this fog is thick," Gwen said.

"Remember that horror movie *The Fog?* And how, out of the dark fog, came this terrifying—"

"Shut up, Jeffrey, and ride."

We checked out Goggle's first.

Frankenstein's monster hopped off his bike and clamped up to the door in his horseshoe boots. I heard a little kid across the street scream, "Horses! I hear horses, Mummy!"

Goggle's was empty, except for Mr. Goggle, who sat at the counter drinking something pink. Kaybee wasn't there.

We rode on. We peeked inside the Red Rooster Restaurant, then the Page After Page Bookstore and even the Pin Bin Bowling Alley. No Kaybee. We zoomed to the Zoo. It was closed.

"Now the railway station," I said. "If she's not there, we'll check her house."

"Gotcha, pard," Gwen said.

We turned our bikes round and roared towards the station.

We'd only ridden two blocks when out of the fog to our right came a green lizard two metres high, all wet and slimy-looking.

"My gosh!" Gwen said, swerving away from it.

"Hi, guys!" said a muffled voice from the

lizard.

Then a flap opened in the lizard's throat and a face peered out at us.

"Dave!" I said.

"You scared me silly," Gwen said.

"But you've always been silly," Dave said, yukking. "Hey, you guys are soaked."

"We know, David, we know," Gwen said. "We're out looking for Kaybee. When she left the Zoo, she never went home. She's run away. Seen her?"

"Oh, gee. Yeah, I did. Saw her about, oh, about, oh, about fifteen minutes ago, I guess. Maybe it was more like twenty."

"Well, where is she?" I screamed.

"Hey, no need to get mad," Dave said. "I know you're probably mad at me for not sticking up for you at the Zoo today. I mean, Kaybee must feel rotten. No wonder she ran away. I'm really sorry about that. It's just that—"

"David," Gwen snapped. "We have to know where Kaybee is. Now where did you see her?"

"She was heading that way." He nodded off to the right with his huge lizard head. "Towards the railway station. She had a large paper bag with her. I thought she was out trick-or-treating, but maybe her clothes were in the bag because she's running away. What do you think?"

"I think," I said, "that we've got to get to that railway station, and get there *fast!*"

"Right!" Gwen yelled.

"Thanks, Dave!" I hollered as we sped off.

"I doubt if I can keep up with you," Dave hollored back. "I can hardly move inside this stupid lizard!"

My legs were killing me. The horseshoes I'd nailed onto the old work boots were too heavy for my aching thighs.

"Hurry!" Gwen yelled, pulling ahead of me.

"I'm trying, I'm trying!"

I pedalled really hard three times, then coasted, then pedalled, then coasted. That helped a lot.

Until I got a flat tyre.

Pop—sssssssss-s-s-s-s

"Gwen!" I shouted. But she rode on, not noticing I'd stopped. She disappeared into the fog bank ahead.

"Jeff?" I heard her yell from within the fog.

"Back here! Got a puncture!"

"Darn! Just what we need," Gwen said as she skidded to a halt beside me.

"Let em sit on your handlebars," I said.

"I can't steer that way."

"Then *I'll* drive, you ride on the handelbars. Move it."

We left my bike hidden in some bushes, and soon we were wobbling down the road. Frankenstein's monster was pedalling with his throbbing legs, and the fairy princess was riding high on the handlebars with rainwater dripping off her golden hair into the monster's face.

Soon Gwen yelled, "There it is!"

Up ahead, through the swirling fog, I saw the dim yellow lights of the railway station. Next door was a small, greasy cafe that some of the kids liked to hang out in because it had a few video games and played rock music all the time.

We slid to a halt, tipped over, crashed to the ground, scrambled to our feet, and ran into the station.

A train was just chugging out.

"Oh, no!" Gwen said.

"Do you think she was on that train?" I asked.

"I don't know. Kaybee's not here now. The whole station is empty."

I yelled, "Kaybee-bee-bee-bee!" My echoes boomed round the station and died out. No one answered.

"Darn," Gwen said. We wandered out of the station towards her bike.

Just then, I saw five or six people run out of the cafe next door. They were racing towards us. Before I knew what was happening, I felt a hand shove me on the chest. Staring at me in the face was large-as-a-bull Crunch McFink. With him was Pinky and a few of her stocky friends.

"Well, well, well," Pinky said. "Look who we have here, Crunch. Your two favourite kids in all the world."

"Hrrrrr," said Crunch.

"Beat it," Gwen said.

"Yeah," I added.

Pinky shoved me. "Listen, Franken-nerd, I don't like how you talked to me at the Zoo today."

"Tough," I said. "I didn't like what you did to Kaybee."

Crunch shoved me again. "Talk nice now," he growled.

"Listen, you creeps," Gwen said, "we're looking for Kaybee. No one's seen her since she ran out of the Zoo. She's disappeared and she could be in big trouble. Her folks are going to call the police if we don't find her. Have you seen her?"

Pinky and Crunch and the other girls exchanged happy glances.

"Awww," Pinky said, "too bad. You just missed her. Five minutes ago she ran into the station and hopped on to that train."

"Rats!" I said. We were too late. The worst had happened.

"Hey," Pinky said to her friends, "maybe Kaybee took the train back to her rocket ship. Maybe she went back to Mars!"

They all laughed.

"Shut up!" I screamed. I shoved Pinky. Hard. She said "Uh!" and stumbled back into her gang.

"Whoa!" Crunch said. He scrunched up the front of my costume in his massive fist and dragged me close to his face. His breath smelled as if he'd been licking garbage cans. "Nobody hits girls with me around," he wheezed.

"Then why don't you leave?" I said.

He grabbed me with his other hand. "You going to make me? Huh? Maybe you and your outer space girlfriend gonna blast me away, huh? Maybe the fairy princess here will turn me into a toad, huh?"

"Too late," I said. "You already are a toad. And if you don't let go, I'm gonna turn you into toad soup!"

I was a maniac now. I'd had it with everything. I'd wrecked Kaybee's life, her parents' lives, and my life. I had nothing to lose. And no fat bully was going to make things worse.

"Ha!" Crunch said into my face. Then he balled up a fist the size of a football and aimed it at my chin.

There was only one thing I could do. I raised my heavy, horseshoe Frankenstein boot and stamped on his foot. Twice.

"Yaaaag!" Crunch screamed, hopping around.

"Get them!" Pinky yelled.

Pinky and her goons attacked. Gwen and I struggled and fought and scratched and kicked, but there were too many of them for us to handle. They soon had our arms pinned behind us. Then they turned us towards Crunch, who looked like he was mad enough to eat us.

This was the end. I knew it.

"Say your prayers," Crunch said. He was flexing his hands.

Pinky was smiling. "This will teach you two to stick up for crazy kids like Kaybee, and this will teach you to mess with us. Did you really believe she was from outer space? You jerk! You really thought you'd convince us it was true, didn't you? You fool! Look what's it got you now, nerd! Get 'em, Crunch!"

Crunch moved towards us, chuckling under his heavy breaths.

Then suddenly he stopped.

Crunch's eyes shrank to slits. He was peering into the murky dark fog over to our right. The yellowish light from the cafe gave the fog an eerie glow. "Thought I saw something moving over there."

"The cops?" Pinky asked.

"Naw, wasn't the cops," Crunch said. "Something else. There! There it is again!"

"What? Where? Huh?" Pinky and her gang said.

"Over there!" Crunch. He was pointing now. "Look!"

"What *is* it?"

I turned to look, then yelped, "Wuh?"

There, floating all by itself in the thick fog, was Kaybee's head. Just her head.

"Hello, earthlings," Kaybee's head said as it bobbed around in the fog.

"Kaybee," Gwen whispered.

"You were right all the time, Jeffrey," Kaybee's head said. "I am not from your planet. I am, in true fact, an alien. You believed me for a while, didn't you?"

"Y-yes," I said.

"But no one else did," Kaybee said. "And that makes me very, very, intensely angry."

"It's a trick," Pinky said. "She got on the train!"

But Pinky began to back away.

Crunch grabbed my arm. "Make her stop. Make her go away. She's weird!"

"Pinky," said Kaybee's head, fading in and out of the fog, "you must now let Jeffrey and Gwendolyn go. And you must do it immediately. Or I may have to use my amazing alien power to make your hair disappear completely."

Pinky's hands went to her head. "Oh, yeah? Hey! Where'd she go?"

Kaybee's head was gone. All our heads were twisting this way and that, trying to find her.

My heart was hammering. *Had I been right all along?*

"Hello, again," Kaybee said.

Now she was behind us. And her head was on the ground!

"Better get going now, Pinky," Kaybee's head said. "You didn't believe I was an alien before, but you had better believe it now. Awful things can happen to Earth girls who do not believe."

For a few moments Pinky couldn't do anything. She was frozen with wide-eyed fear.

"She is an alien!" Crunch screamed.

Then Kaybee vanished. She soon appeared like a ghost about ten metres in front of us. "I'm get-ting ang-ry," Kaybee's head sang.

"Crunch—" Pinky said. But when she looked around, Crunch was gone. We could hear his running footsteps echoing as he raced down the road.

Then Pinky's friends sped off.

Pinky looked back to where Kaybee had been, but Kaybee's head was gone. In its's place, just emerging from the fog, was a gigantic lizard.

"Sh-she turned into a dinosaur!" Pinky screeched. She quicky turned to me, knees shaking. "Jeff, you have to protect me from her? You—"

Suddenly a hand appeared behind Pinky. A finger tapped her on the shoulder..

Slowly, very slowly, Pinky turned her head round to look. Kaybee's head was a centimetre from Pinky's face.

"*Go!*" Kaybee screamed.

Pinky yelped, twirled around twice, then took off like a bullet.

That left me and Gwen. I had closed my eyes when Kaybee had shouted. Now I was slowly opening them.

There was Kaybee. Surrounding her was a wide, fluffy, grey, and gauzy thing.

Kaybee smiled. "My super fog costume works extremely well, yes?"

EIGHTEEN

We couldn't stop laughing. The owner of the cafe came out to see what all the racket was about, and what he saw must have been pretty strange: Frankenstein's monster, a fairy princess, a giant lizard, and a puff of fog bumping into each other and howling into the drizzly night. The owner stood there for a minute, then simply turned round, closed the cafe door, put up the CLOSED sign, and turned off the lights. That got us laughing even harder.

When we finally got tired of laughing, we just hung around and wheezed.

"Kaybee, I'm really sorry," I said. "Really, I mean it, I mean it a lot."

"We were worried about you," Gwen said. "We thought we'd never find you."

"I didn't mean any of it," I said. "I'm sorry. I want to be your friends again. I really do. I'm sorry for all I did. I didn't know what the heck I was doing. I'm sorry."

"Jeffrey, Gwendolyn," Kaybee said, "do not

worry. We are still friends. I saw how worried you were when you came here to seek me. I saw how you were going to battle to the death with that horrible Pinky and her mean friends and that blubber-butt Crunch. Did you see how they ran?"

"Yeah," I said, "it was great!"

"They-they-they," Dave said, taking off his lizard head. "Those jerks thought Kaybee was an alien! They thought I was a dinosaur!"

We all burst out laughing again.

"Kaybee," Gwen said, "where were you all day? Where did you go? We thought you got on that train."

"Oh, it's not a happy story," she said. "I guess I am more mixed-up than even I thought I was."

What kind of job did Mr Keeper have with the government? How can any *human* read as fast as Kaybee?.

"We heard about your being adopted and everything," Gwen said. "Your folks were really worried. They came over to Jeff's and we listened in."

"I'm glad you know," Kaybee said. "At the Zoo today I thought I had once again moved to a place where people hate me. I was so terribly sad and upset that my friend Jeffrey was making fun of me. I just wanted to get away, to run away, to be away somewhere. So I walked for ages. But where would I go? I wondered. Last time I ran away I tried to find my real parents.

That was silly, I know, because they do no even know me. So this time I didn't think where to go!"

"I'm really sorry, really sorry," I said.

"It's all right," Kaybee said. "I know you are a good person, Jeffrey. And while I was walking, that is what I was thinking. I was thinking that you were a good person all along, Jeffrey. You, too, Gwendolyn. Then I thought: But if they are good, why am I so sad? Then I knew that that awful Pinky Nickle was the one who always started all my troubles. Other kids who didn't like me just stayed away from me, but Pinky wanted to see me cry all the time. It was good for me to think this, because I knew right then that I still had friends. But then I could not let Pinky do this to me and my friends any more. I had to teach her the ultimate lesson. So I went home and no one was there—I guess Mummer and Dadder were at your house, Jeffrey—and I got the fog costume I had been making for weeks. It looks just like fog, doesn't it?"

"It's great," I said.

"So I went to Pinky's house, and when she left, I followed her here. But she saw me, so I ran into the station. I heard her say to her friends that I had got on the train. Then I didn't know what to do until I saw you and Gwendolyn come and get into trouble with them. I was hoping to blend into the fog and scare them—and it worked! And David, you

143

came at just the right millisecond!"

"I did, didn't I?" Dave said, bouncing up and down on his long lizard toes.

"I think I should go home now," Kaybee said. "Mummer and Dadder must be very worried."

"Good idea," Gwen said. "We'll go with you. Dave, you want to come?"

"Don't think so," he said. "Gotta get back home. Kaybee, I'm sorry too. I won't make fun of you any more, I promise."

"Thank you, David. You are a funny person."

Dave smiled. "I can't wait for school on Monday. The whole place will be laughing at Pinky and Crunch for years!"

"I'll make sure of that!" I said. "See ya, Dave."

"Bye," said Gwen and Kaybee.

And Dave, with his lizard head under his arm, slowly shuffled into the fog and disappeared.

So, despite everything, Kaybee stayed my friend. I felt proud.

We picked up my bike by the bushes and headed to Kaybee's house.

Mr. and Mrs. Keeper were so happy to see Kaybee that they hugged her until Kaybee had to beg them to stop. Even Sneeze stopped sneezing long enough to give Kaybee a few juicy licks. The Keepers called up my folks, told them the good news, then invited them over.

Soon everyone, including Joey, who immediately fell in love with Sneeze, were sitting around the Keepers' living room sipping hot apple cider and listening to us tell them how we found Kaybee.

When we were done, Mrs. Keeper said to Kaybee, "We are very proud of you, dear. You didn't really run away. You stayed and were loyal to your friends. Now you know you *do* have friends. Nice friends. Good friends. Friends who really care about you."

"I know I do," Kaybee said. "But—"

"But what, honey?" Mr. Keeper asked.

"But I—I do not know what to do with all the other kids in school. I mean, I don't know how to be around them, how to act."

"Just be yourself," Mrs. Keeper said.

"But, Mummer, I don't know how to do that! I get all confused and upset!"

"Is that why you try to be so, well, so different?" my dad asked.

Kaybee nodded. "I think so. But I really don't know." Kaybee looked at her Mummer and Dadder. "Can't you tell me how to act? Can't you show me? You never say *anything!*" And Kaybee started crying.

Mrs. Keeper lookd at Mr. Keeper. She said in a quiet voice, "She's right, we haven't been doing anything much to help her. We just let her do whatever she wants to do."

Mr. Keeper patted his wife on the arm, then spoke to Kaybee. "From now on, Kaybee everything's going to be different. We'll help you, and you can help us, too."

"And you can come over to our house anytime," my mum said.

"And if anyone ever bothers you at school," I said, "Wham! To the moon!

"And that goes double for me!" Gwen said.

"And I'll never run away again," Kaybee said. Then she thought for a second and frowned. "Does this mean I have to stop painting my pictures and looking at the stars and ..." Tears sprang again from her eyes.

"Absolutely not," her father said. "You love doing those things, and everybody should do what they love doing. As a matter of fact, let's frame a couple of your pictures and hang them in the living room!"

Mrs. Keeper gave Mr. Keeper a raised-eyebrows look.

"Well," he said, "maybe in the den."

Everybody laughed and Sneeze sneezed and Joey sneezed with him.

Mrs. Keeper gave us all some more apple cider, and everybody chatted back and forth for a while. During all the talking I found out a few interesting facts. First, the Keepers used to live in New Jersey. They said talking about it made them remember how bad things were there, so they didn't like even to think about it. Second, Mr. Keeper used to work for the Draft Board in Dover, New Jersey. That was his government job. He showed me the terrific gold digital watch they'd given him when he retired. Its alarm played "Happy Days Are Here Again".

Soon it was getting late, and we said goodbye. We told Kaybee we'd see her at the bus stop on Monday. Gwen took off on her bike, and Mum and Dad loaded my bike into the boot of the car and we drove home.

On the way home Mum and Dad didn't say anything about me running out of the house against their orders. Dad did, however, scream at me for getting wet: I was wearing Dad's work boots.

NINETEEN

RING-A-DING-A-CLANG-CLANG. The bell rang for the start of school on Monday. Pinky and Crunch hadn't shown up yet, and Kaybee, Gwen and Dave, and I had spent the last fifteen minutes telling everybody how the two dumbos had been scared out of their pants Halloween night because they thought Kaybee was an alien from outer space. The class was buzzing, and everybody kept looking towards the door waiting for Crunch and Pinky—for years Crunch and Pinky had been picking on everybody, and this was our once-in-a-lifetime chance to get back.

Poor Mrs. Binker couldn't shut us up.

"Quiet! Quiet! Quiet!" she screamed, and whack, whack, whack, went her ruler.

Just when the class was finally calming down, Pinky and Crunch walked in, and the class broke up.

Pinky was blushing and Crunch had a look on his face like he'd just sat on a nail. It was obvious that they had already heard that: one,

Kaybee was not an alien from outer space, and two, that they were the biggest fools of the school.

"Hey!" someone yelled at Pinky, "seen any UFO's lately?"

The class roared.

Mrs. Binker's ruler whacked, then broke in half.

"Crunch! Crunch!" someone else bellowed. "Watch out for the fog monster!"

The class thundered.

Mrs. Binker stamped her foot, winced, then sat down to rub it.

Pinky and Crunch crawled to their seats, then slithered down as far as they could go.

Finally Mrs. Binker managed to quieten everyone down by slamming a fat dictionary on her desk top about twenty times.

"That's better," she said. "Now." She turned around to write something on the blackboard.

When Kaybee leaned over to Crunch, the whole class turned to listen.

"Psst. Crunch," Kaybee said. "I am very sorry to have played such a rotten trick on you."

"Yeah?"

"Yes. I am really not from outer space. It was just my strangeness coming out. I am as normal as you are." She turned away, then turned back. "I mean, everybody can walk through walls can't they?"

Crunch's eyes flew wide open, and the class

exploded. And I was laughing hardest of all.

Some other Hippo Books to look out for:

THE DANCING METEORITE
Ann Mason

0 590 70541 5   £1.50

Kira Warden is the most talented E-Comm in the system. She can chat to any alien in any language in the system, but science is *not* her strong point. But, when Kira sees a dancing meteorite she knows enough to realize that she has seen the impossible! And a moving meteorite could destroy the whole space station!

Kira *has* to warn them!

ALIENS IN THE FAMILY
Margaret Mahy

0 590 70557 1   £1.50

Bond is in trouble. He is being chased, and his pursuers are powerful and dangerous. When Dora, Lewis and Jake help him, he's grateful, but fears for their safety. Getting Bond to a lonely place beyond the city turns into a far greater adventure than any of the children dream of, but even when lonely, defensive Jake guesses the truth, they are all the more determined to succeed.

Time Twister
Ged Maybury
0 590 70587 3   £1.50

When Jason, Helena and Troy play "Time Twister" they discover that they can time travel! But soon they are forced to use their skills to combat the wrong course of time. The future depends on them!